"Your husband is dead!" he snapped

The detective stared relentlessly at Laura. "And that poisoning was no accident. It was in the glass of water you gave him."

"No!" she screamed in denial, frantic fear rising in her. "I didn't love my husband, but I would never have...." Laura fell silent as she realized her impossible situation.

She was alone, without friends, in a strange country...and all the evidence pointed to her. She'd never be able to defend herself against the charge of murder!

Other

MYSTIQUE BOOKS

by MAGALI

For a free catalogue listing all available Mystique Books,
send your name and address to:

MYSTIQUE BOOKS,
M.P.O. Box 707, Niagara Falls, N.Y. 14302
In Canada: 649 Ontario St., Stratford, Ontario N5A 6W2

The Deadly Pawn

by MAGALI

▟▙ MYSTIQUE BOOKS

TORONTO • LONDON • NEW YORK

HAMBURG • AMSTERDAM • STOCKHOLM

THE DEADLY PAWN / first published July 1980

ISBN 0-373-50088-2

PRINTED IN U.S.A.

Chapter 1

Shortly after ten o'clock on a sunny Thursday morning, a young woman hurried along the peaceful Paris sidewalks. The streets were deserted—the rush hour was over and businessmen were safely ensconced in their office armchairs; soon the housewives would finish their second cup of coffee, and then the streets would again be full of life.

The young woman turned down a side street and entered a large, airy apartment building. Entering an apartment on the ground floor, she slammed the door behind her. She called out to her roommate and heard a sleepy yawn.

"Back from work already?" Sonia asked as she sat up in bed, rubbing the sleep from her eyes.

"Only for a minute. I have to leave again right away," the young woman answered. "I have to pack a suit-case—I'm going to the Riviera!" She dropped her purse and peeled off her suede coat, draping it carelessly over a chair. "But first I'm going to make some coffee. Want a cup?"

The young woman disappeared into the kitchen while Sonia halfheartedly dragged herself out of bed. She shoved her feet into a pair of blue slippers, shrugged on a housecoat and shuffled into the kitchen after her roommate.

Laura Dolan was plugging in the percolator when Sonia appeared. "How's your cold? Any better?" Laura asked.

Sonia leaned against the door frame, wiggling her toes in the blue slippers. "Not a sneeze left," she answered, "but don't tell my boss. I thought I could use an extra day off." She flopped across the kitchen in the slippers, which were several sizes too large. "Why the rush to the Riviera?" she asked, as she set two cups and a pitcher of cream on the table.

"Boss's orders," Laura replied happily. "The fitter who was supposed to go—Agnes—ran into a wall last night."

"Typical woman driver!" Sonia laughed. "I hope she wasn't hurt."

"Her arm is in a cast . . . hardly the way to represent the Leonardo studios at a high-society wedding."

"But you're not going to oversee the fitting, are you? I mean, granted, you designed all those elegant monstrosities . . . but what are you going to do if any adjustments have to be made?"

"Well . . . to tell you the truth, I'm just praying that everything fits. But just in case, I'm taking Zizi of the nimble fingers. She's as dizzy as a leaf—but you should see her at work! She'll be able to fix anything that needs fixing." Laura poured the coffee, delighting in its familiar early-morning smell. The spring sun beamed through the kitchen window, brightening everything in its path. Laura looked around peacefully. It was nice to be home in the middle of the morning, she decided. It was a rare freedom for her—she was usually hard at work in her office at Leonardo's by eight-thirty. This was almost as good as a day off—better, she thought, because of the free trip to the Riviera. It would be nice to spend her days rushing around the country, attending society weddings, hobnobbing with foreign ministers and chic women. . . . Sonia's voice interrupted her daydreams.

"Laura—happy birthday! I almost forgot about it. Speaking of birthdays, weren't you supposed to be celebrating with Ross tonight?"

"I've already called him; he's taking me to the station."

"Did he throw a fit?"

"No more than usual."

"Sure, sure, you've got him wrapped around your little finger," Sonia said lightly. "You're lucky, Laura . . . Ross always forgives you. But one of these days he's going to give up on you and your world traveling," she teased.

"World traveler I'm not—but it sure would be nice, wouldn't it? Imagine, changing planes in Rome . . . hopping a jet to Athens . . . a few days in Venice once or twice a month . . . . Fat chance, though," Laura said wistfully. "Usually Leonardo has me chained to my desk. But for today I'm free—at least until Ross gets here to pick me up. I'd better get moving or I won't be ready."

THERE WAS VERY LITTLE about Laura Dolan that was conventional. On the surface, perhaps, her life was bounded by convention. She had a nine-to-five job, a boyfriend, an apartment with a rocking chair and a toaster, a roommate. Laura did all the normal things—differently.

She'd been born and bred in Paris, and her conservative, middle-class parents had wanted to send her to secretarial school. But their seemingly tractable teenager had rebelled. "There has to be more to life than taking dictation and changing ribbons," Laura had said, and had then enrolled in the Paris School of Design. She graduated with first-class honors and took her knowledge of the haute couture to London, where she developed new styles for fashion-conscious Britons. She had shared a cold-water walk-up apartment with five girls—and had loved it.

Her first year in London was heaven and she had been anticipating another equally happy year until, without warning, her father had died. Although she'd lived away from home for almost five years, Laura was close to her family. She was heartbroken at her father's death and immediately moved back to Paris to try to fill the gap in her mother's life.

Laura had never had any trouble finding a job, and shortly after her return to France she started working at Leonardo's, one of the most chic fashion houses in the city. Through some friends she had met Sonia, and the two women had decided to pool their resources so they could live in the center of the city without risking financial ruin.

The arrangement was working well. Laura kept her boyfriend's visits to a minimum, and in exchange for putting up with Ross occasionally, Sonia had the place to herself one weekend out of four, when Laura went to visit her mother.

Mrs. Dolan, much to her chagrin, was no longer liv-

ing in Paris. She was the somewhat less-than-proud
owner of a beautiful cottage in Belleville, on the banks
of the Marne River. The cottage had been chosen and
purchased by Laura's father. He had been looking forward to his retirement, and had decided that he would
spend it in the country. He'd enjoyed only a few months
of his idyllic dream before he died. His widow missed
him, and she missed the city, too.

But she couldn't afford Paris. So she resigned herself
to her fate, inviting her sister, a retired school teacher,
to share that fate with her. She had begun to enjoy
country life—although she'd never admit it—and was
always involved in some crazy scheme or other. One
week she might refuse to cook anything except what
came from her garden or the river; another week she
was an ardent conservationist, refusing to drive so as
not to waste fossil fuel. She enjoyed her daughter's
visits—and so did Laura, who took pleasure in her
mother's continual surprises.

Laura's only complaint about her visits to Belleville
was that they took her away from Ross. Ross approved
of Laura's concern for her family; at the same time, he
missed her when she was away. Because of their
schedules, they rarely saw each other during the week.
Laura's job kept her busy all day, and Ross worked until
midnight, often later. He really liked his job, so he
didn't resent the hours he put in, and his dedication was
beginning to pay off.

He had started working for the television station as a
copy boy. In six years he had been promoted as many
times; he had recently been made a reporter-
broadcaster, and Laura teased him about being just
another pretty face. A lot of people at the station said

seriously that Ross Montclair had personally doubled the news audience—adding that all the new viewers were, of course, female.

Ross and Laura had known each other since they were kids. Ross spent the first ten years of their relationship ignoring Laura. Then he turned sixteen and fell in love with her. He'd been faithful ever since. Laura had conducted a few elementary romantic experiments with other men while she was in Britain, but the results had led her unerringly back to Ross. Although she had as many admirers as her boyfriend had, she ignored them. When she stopped arguing with Ross long enough to think about it, she realized their relationship was a solid one.

THE TRAIN WAS WAITING at the platform when Ross and Laura arrived at the station. Zizi of the nimble fingers, Laura's assistant for this trip, was waiting in the doorway of one of the cars. When she spotted Laura she began waving her arms like a windmill. She looked like a caricature of the typical tourist—camera in hand, flash attachment hanging from the camera strap, light meter around her neck.

"How come you're dressed up like a cameraman?" Ross asked her teasingly.

"It's my first trip ever to the Riviera, and I intend to take advantage of the occasion—I've got three rolls of film!"

"You won't have much time for taking pictures," Laura said doubtfully. "Don't forget we're going down there to work."

"Once the bride's all dressed, we'll have plenty of time to poke around the town."

"Hold on, now!" Ross protested, laughing. "You can't stay down there forever—I want Laura back."

"Don't worry, Mr. Montclair. I'll take care of your Laura and bring her back as fast as I can. But the way I figure it, this trip is going to be fun, and I intend to have a good time. After all, how long can it take to make sure a dress fits?"

Laura did her best to look authoritative and disapproving, but she had to laugh at her irrepressible companion.

Zizi put on an innocent face and disappeared, leaving Ross and Laura to say their goodbyes. She glanced back once: her co-worker and the reporter were locked in an embrace, oblivious to the bustle on the platform. She smiled and went off to find the newspaper vendor to buy her favorite magazine, the one that revealed the love lives of the stars.

Zizi walked slowly back to her car, contemplating the best way to answer a promise of everlasting love from Robert Redford. As she waltzed along, totally bemused, she almost bumped into a tall, nicely dressed man. He was standing motionless on the platform, blocking the doorway to the car, staring intently at Laura.

He's handsome, Zizi thought, *but he's got his nerve.* Never one to be bashful or retiring, Zizi unleashed her gamin tongue on the stranger. "Well, what are you waiting for? In or out, if you please! Make up your mind! You're not on your own front porch."

The man turned his eyes slowly to Zizi; on his face was a look of surprise and intense interest. Without a word, he disappeared into the railroad car.

Zizi was quite pleased with her successful defense of Laura. She looked for her companion to tell her about the incident and spotted the man staring through the window, his nose practically pressed against the glass. His gaze was fixed intently on Laura's face.

Another victim of love, Zizi decided. She gave Laura an admiring look, untainted by jealousy. Laura *was* attractive, there was no doubt about that. Zizi considered herself to be an expert in such matters. After all, she was surrounded by fashion models all day at Leonardo's, and she studied the movie magazines voraciously in her spare time. She looked at her companion critically. Laura might not be considered beautiful in a conventional way, but she was beautiful. Her high cheekbones, generous mouth and widely spaced blue eyes, along with her shoulder-length auburn hair set her apart from the crowd. Zizi's impish eyes lit up as she thought of the love-struck stranger.

As soon as the two women were settled in their compartment and before Laura had a chance to get thoroughly involved in her newspaper, Zizi announced, "You conquered another man's heart. While you were on the platform I noticed a guy who couldn't keep his eyes off you."

"Are you sure he was looking at me and not Ross?"

"Why would a man be staring at Ross?"

"A lot of people do—it's because he's on TV. They know they've seen him somewhere but they can't remember where."

"I'm sure this man was looking at you. He was drinking you in—with thirsty eyes, as they say in all the love stories."

Laura looked slyly at Zizi. "I suppose you gave him a piece of your mind after you finished gaping at him," she teased.

"Of course I did," Zizi responded. "You didn't expect me to let his rudeness pass unnoticed, did you?" Laura laughed and opened her newspaper and Zizi turned to the window. She was soon entranced by the countryside flashing by. She was strictly a city girl; her horizon was marked by the wall of the apartment building across the street, and her version of wild country was a hedge in a Paris park. The vista from the train window was a revelation, and Zizi half expected a zebra to come crashing through the suburban greenery.

While Zizi was being held in thrall by the French countryside, Laura had abandoned her newspaper and was thinking about her schedule. She'd promised Saturday to Ross—but this weekend was the one to visit her mother. Laura didn't want to miss the trip to Belleville, and she knew her mother would be disappointed, too. Her life was beginning to feel a little bit hectic.

The steward from the dining car came down the aisle, ringing his little brass bell. "Restaurant tickets for the first sitting," he called.

"I'll take you to lunch," Laura offered, glad to take advantage of the chance to forget her problems for an hour or two.

Eager to oblige, Zizi took her up on the offer. They made their way to the dining car, where a mixture of rich aromas greeted them.

Zizi took her place in the booth across from Laura. The waiter appeared with the wine list and Zizi went into raptures—she'd never had wine on a train before, she told Laura excitedly. Then she opened the menu and her face lit up. She couldn't help bursting out, "Laura, we'll be eating like kings! Veal *cordon bleu!*"

As her happy voice reached the upper registers, the

other diners turned to glance at her with amused looks.

"Zizi!" Laura hissed through her laughter. "Calm down—everybody's staring."

Zizi immediately put on her innocent face. "So?" she asked imperturbably.

"What do you mean, so, you goof. I can't take you anywhere," Laura giggled.

"Oh, really," Zizi said disdainfully, trying unsuccessfully to mask the irrepressible sparkle in her eyes. "Well, madam, my apologies, indeed."

Laura decided to let Zizi win that round. She turned her attention to the waiter who was hovering at her shoulder, ready to take their order.

Zizi managed to contain herself until their food arrived, content with an occasional comment on the train, the scenery, the handsome waiters, the mustache the chef was cultivating, the apparel of their fellow diners. . . .

"There's no hope for you, Zizi," Laura interrupted her. "You're an incurable romantic. And by the way, if you use that fork for the fish, you won't have anything to eat your dessert with."

"If it isn't Amy Vanderbilt herself, the Queen of Etiquette!" Zizi retorted, laughing.

The two women laughed their way through lunch and Laura realized, during her second glass of wine, that she hadn't been this relaxed during a workday since . . . . She couldn't remember when. The realization startled her. She hadn't thought about the daily routine of her life in a long time, but now she saw that the pressures in the studio were beginning to tell on her. She tried to be objective about the situation, to figure out exactly what was wrong. She wasn't sure—but she knew it had been a few months since she had looked forward to going into the studio in the morning.

Still thinking seriously, Laura paid for the lunch and headed down the train, her companion close behind her. As she entered their compartment, Laura noticed that she had lost Zizi somewhere along the way. *Maybe she stopped at the ladies' room*, Laura thought, and went back to her musings about her job.

There was nothing specific she could complain about at Leonardo's. She had a good job and a pleasant office. True, it had been a long time since she had been given a raise, or a promotion. . . . *Or a change*, Laura thought suddenly. *I'm bored*. She looked out the window at the passing scenery, wondering what to do with her discovery. As the train wound its way through the early spring countryside, Laura grew increasingly depressed.

Suddenly Zizi burst into the compartment, her cheeks flushed and her eyes full of mischief.

"I knew he was after you," she announced mysteriously, dropping into her seat.

"After me? Who?"

"The voyeur—the man who was staring at you back on the platform."

"Zizi, calm down. Begin at the beginning. What are you talking about?"

"Well, I was following you back here after lunch and I saw him again," Zizi said, trying to keep the excitement from her voice.

"You saw him . . . and then what happened?"

"He asked me your name."

"Oh, terrific," Laura said tiredly. "What do you think he wants? Where was he, anyway? I didn't notice anything."

"He was in the dining car, but he was sitting behind you. When I started to follow you, he came up behind me and stopped me in the passageway. I was about to tell him exactly what I thought of him, but he was as polite as could be."

Suddenly Zizi screwed up her face, put one hand on her heart and flung her other hand out in an exaggerated gesture. " 'Miss, I entreat you, one question, please. I would like to know if the lady across from you at luncheon was Delia Marston, the actress.'

"Naturally—" Zizi reverted to her normal voice "—I could hardly believe my ears. Then I had an idea—I asked him if that was why he had been staring at you so hard just before the train left. He was on the platform, remember?

"This gentleman answers, 'Please forgive me, miss, but I do want to talk to Delia Marston.'

" 'Too bad,' I told him. 'She's Laura Dolan, not Delia Marston.' "

" 'Are you sure?' "

" 'Of course I'm sure. She works where I do, at the Leonardo Studios in Paris. Haven't you heard of them?' " Zizi put on her most disgusted look and added, "He hadn't even heard of the Leonardo Studios. He must really be out to lunch!"

She leaned back in her seat, obviously enjoying the story, and reported more of her encounter. "He couldn't get Delia Marston out of his mind; he tried to convince me that's who you really were. Imagine that! I told him who you were again, and I swore you'd never set foot on a stage. Finally he gave up and wandered off somewhere, maybe to think about his precious Delia Marston. But I don't think so—if you want to know my opinion, that's just a line. He's a fallen for you. It was written all over his face. But just in case he got any brilliant ideas, I thought of a way to keep him away from you—I told him you were engaged. That shut him up fast."

"You're a little ahead of yourself," Laura reminded her. "I'm not engaged."

"You might as well be."

"That doesn't matter. . . . Are you sure Ross didn't pay you to say all these nice things about him?"

Zizi giggled. "Are you kidding? Boy, that would be something. Ross Montclair, ace reporter, doing business with me! He's—he's almost a star. One of these days he might even be in my magazine!"

"Sure, Zizi . . . they're going to make him famous, right?" Laura laughed. Then her face grew serious. "But what about this man on the train? What did he look like?"

"Not bad . . . he looks sort of like a tough guy. Tender tough, I'd say. You know what I mean?"

Laura smiled. "The perfect seducer."

"Well, maybe in the movies, but he's not my type. He's too old—and besides, he's got an accent."

"An accent? What kind?"

"A foreign accent . . . I couldn't tell from where."

"Well, it doesn't really matter. I think we should close the door, though—I don't want him prowling around here. I've got a lot of things I want to think about."

Laura curled up on her seat and closed her eyes. Zizi, beginning to enjoy this encounter with a stranger, decided to stand guard. From time to time she pressed her nose against the glass door but the curious man didn't show his face.

It was late that evening when they arrived at their hotel in Nice, and both Laura and Zizi were grateful that all they had to do was curl up in their beds in their hotel room. They would both have to be up early the next morning in order to arrange the final touches for the wedding, and working with people in an emotional turmoil was never easy. Laura thought wryly to herself that she wouldn't get much of a holiday out of this trip, for they would be returning to Paris on the overnight train the next evening after the ceremony. But as she snuggled up against her pillow, she consoled herself with the thought that at least it was a change from her usual routine.

THE WEDDING WAS the ultimate in sumptuous luxury. Everything had been meticulously planned, down to the last flower, and the arrangements were flawless. After the church ceremony there was a reception at the bride's father's villa, which was perched high atop Mount Boron. The city of Nice lay hundreds of feet below, like a jewel nestled in the curve of the bay.

The gowns Laura had designed were admired endlessly, and both Laura and Zizi were invited to the reception. Zizi took advantage of her opportunity and tasted every hors d'oeuvre she could find. Laura remained quietly in the background, occasionally acknowledging the praise her gowns were attracting.

After the reception Laura was exhausted. She declined Zizi's invitation to explore the city, and instead returned to her hotel room to curl up in the big bed. She read two pages of one of Zizi's magazines and then drifted off to sleep. When she awoke with a start it was dark outside and Zizi had not returned. Laura glanced at her watch and leaped out of bed. She'd have to hurry or she'd miss her train. In a panic, she began throwing everything into her bag haphazardly. She glanced around the room: Zizi's things were scattered everywhere. She turned back to her own bag and was just trying to zip it shut when Zizi catapulted into the room.

"Zizi, we're going to miss our train!" Laura shouted. "What happened? Where have you been?"

"I got lost," Zizi explained, trying to catch her breath. "What a town! It's so crowded! But the sea is beautiful—like a picture. And I went exploring in the old city. The streets are narrow, and they hang their laundry between their balconies. Friday must be laundry day in Nice—I saw all these women hanging up their sheets."

Zizi attacked her suitcase, dumping everything into it and jamming it closed. Then Laura grabbed her arm and together they ran out of the hotel and down the street to the train station, where they waved their tickets at the guard by the barrier and raced down the steps to the platform just as the train was about to lurch into motion. An attendant was perched on the steps, waiting for last-minute arrivals, and he helped the two women onto the train as the final "All aboard!" was echoing along the platform. With a frightening clack, the door slammed behind them.

They found their way to an empty compartment and sat back, gasping for breath. For a few moments they sat quietly, listening to the comforting noise of the train as it carried them back to Paris. But Zizi couldn't sit still for very long; even after an exhausting day her liveliness bubbled over. She rushed off to find something to drink and brought back coffee for them both. They sat staring into the darkness, drinking quietly.

"By the way," Zizi said suddenly, "I saw that man again. You know, the one from the train to Nice."

"Again? I think it's you he's following, not me."

"Can I help it if I keep running into him? And anyway, this time he was with someone—a blonde."

"A blonde, eh?" Laura teased. "Too bad, Zizi. I guess there's no hope for you."

"The blonde doesn't bother me—she's too old to keep him much longer. But she was holding onto him pretty tight." Zizi stifled a laugh and added, "I took their picture as they were coming out of a jeweler's shop."

"You did? Didn't they mind?"

"They didn't even notice me. They were too busy looking into each other's eyes. Just think of it—a couple of middle-aged turtle doves. Anyway, it's not against the law to take someone's picture, so they didn't have too much choice," Zizi said, a note of finality in her voice. She placed her empty coffee cup on the window ledge and turned her attention to the sometimes tricky task of preparing for sleep on a speeding, swaying train. Laura followed her lead and, a short time later, turned out the light.

Chapter 2

Laura was exhausted after her trip to Nice. She had worked hard while she was there, and her professional duties had kept her from relaxing during the ceremony itself. Her sleep had been interrupted by worry as well. She had returned to Paris feeling tired and unhappy with the world.

She wasn't really sure what was wrong. She liked her job—she enjoyed designing clothes and loved being at the center of the busy fashion world. Her job gave her a chance to watch, and occasionally envy, the rich and elegant women who came to Leonardo's for their wardrobes. It was as close as she'd ever get, Laura thought wistfully, to a life of luxury and ease.

She was worried about her relationship with Ross, too. He was charming, attentive—but not rich. Laura knew he was ambitious, and that he had made up his mind to go places at the station, but sometimes she thought he wasn't moving fast enough to suit her. She didn't know what was wrong . . . any woman should be happy with Ross. But she wasn't any woman, and at the moment she wasn't happy.

Somehow they always seemed to be having problems. True, when they weren't fighting life was wonderful. But lately they seemed to disagree all the time. When Laura wanted a quiet evening, Ross was keen on a night on the town; the nights he came home exhausted, wanting to relax, Laura wanted to paint Paris pink.

Their timing was equally bad where major issues were concerned. There was a time when Laura had been crazy to get married, settle down. That was when she found out how ambitious Ross was. He wanted to devote his life to his career, to be the best reporter the station had ever seen. Now he was a reporter, he'd achieved his first goal, and he began to consider getting married. But Laura had now caught his ambition and was a dedicated career woman.

I'll never be able to figure it out, Laura thought as she unpacked her suitcase. *The whole thing is just too complicated*. What she really wanted to do, she thought, hanging up her silk blouse, was to stay home for a day or two. She wanted to relax, putter around the apartment, maybe watch a movie on TV. But she had promised to visit her mother. Although she wasn't in the mood for another trip, Laura knew how much the visits meant to her mother, so she decided to go.

But this weekend there was another problem. Because of her trip to Nice she'd had to break a date with Ross, so she had promised to see him for dinner on Saturday. Laura realized she'd have to put him off again—and she didn't look forward to the prospect. For all her complaining, she loved Ross and hated to disappoint him.

Ross didn't make things easy for her—he was furious. To him the problem was quite simple: Laura had promised to be in two places at once, and now she was telling him it was impossible. He would never ask her to disappoint her mother, but his anger was apparent. They quarreled over the telephone, and Laura refused to let Ross drive her to her mother's cottage. She needed time to herself, time to think, to sort out her life. When she said this to Ross, he sarcastically promised her all the time she needed. By the time she left for her mother's place, Laura was totally depressed.

The weather was just as black as her mood. It was one of those rainy, early spring days when not even the promise of new life could compensate for the drizzle and the mud. The train ride didn't improve Laura's mood.

She arrived at her mother's cottage hoping for solace, warmth and a relaxing cup of hot tea. But Mrs. Dolan was on an economy binge and had turned down the heat in the cottage. She greeted her daughter, wearing two sweaters and a scarf. The cottage was gloomy and damp; the garden was desolate, beaten into submission by the rain. Laura borrowed a sweater from her mother, but she couldn't seem to get warm. The visit was a disaster.

She returned to Paris on Sunday morning, feeling unhappy with herself and with everyone else. She stayed in the apartment all day, hoping Ross would call, but the phone didn't ring.

ROSS'S WEEKEND was going no better than Laura's. He was worried about their argument—though they often disagreed, he usually managed to keep his temper. But Ross had made up his mind. This once, Laura could apologize to him.

And besides, he was busy. In his desire not to give in to Laura he had planned a week-long trip to Brussels. It would be a working holiday, it was true, but it would get him out of the city and away from Laura. It would give him time to think.

Before he booked his flight, though, he called Laura's apartment. Sonia answered, and told him that Laura was still at the cottage. Ross outlined his plans to Sonia, asking her to pass them on to Laura. Then he called the airport.

He didn't want to lose Laura—there was no doubt in his mind about that. He loved her, no question. But he also knew a week in Brussels would do him good. He'd forbid himself the pleasure of calling Laura during the week, and that would teach her a lesson she'd been needing to learn. From now on, he told himself, the balance of power would swing in his favor.

WITH A GREAT SHOW of formality, Leonardo escorted his visitor to the front door of the shop. It had been an excellent first meeting, he thought to himself, taking another look at his visitor's business card. "Hermes Azopardi," it read; the holder of the card was a buyer for the American firm of Jenkins & Company. Azopardi said he was very interested in the line Leonardo had to offer this season.

With a thoughtful look on his face, Leonardo made his way back to his office. As he passed Laura's workshop, where she sat surrounded by drawings and bits of fabric, he called out, "Could you come and see me in my office?"

A minute later, she sat down at his cluttered desk. Leonardo told her about Azopardi, that he was a buyer from a prosperous American company and that he liked what he'd seen in Leonardo's shop. Then Leonardo hesitated. Despite his businesslike appearance, and despite the obvious prosperity of his shop, Leonardo was not a shrewd businessman. His success was the result of good managers, who ran the shop and hired top-notch designers. Leonardo had little to do with the day-to-day workings of the business and became involved only when a wealthy client asked for him by name. Leonardo didn't know his competition or his clients; he was content to let his managers handle everything. But his visitor this morning had excited him, and he was determined to handle Mr. Azopardi personally. What this client wanted he would get; he had dangled the promise of wealth before Leonardo's greedy eyes, and Leonardo had been dazzled.

As tactfully as he could, Leonardo explained Azopardi's requests to Laura. "Mr. Azopardi is going to order an entire line of new dresses, and I think he'll be setting us up with his American client from now on. But there's even more than that. He came here to hire a designer for the New York firm he represents. Besides their off-the-rack line, they want to start a made-to-measure department. He thinks our collection's fantastic, and he's willing to pay a good price if I let him have the designer who's responsible for it. In other words, you. Now what do you think about that?"

Laura could scarcely believe her ears. A trip to America . . . she had always dreamed about it! She was almost afraid to voice her doubts. "But are you sure the shop can afford to let me go?"

Leonardo gave her a sly smile. "As long as the price is right. Anyway, why would I be against it? First of all, they're paying me to use your services. And second—but only if you agree—I'm counting on you to steer those Americans with their wallets full of dollars right to my door."

"That sounds like conflict of interest to me."

"I prefer to call it the free-enterprise system," Leonardo said with a smile. "We want our clients to get the best quality at the best price."

But Laura still wasn't convinced. "Will they give me a contract?"

"For one year. After that, you can make up your mind if you want to stay."

She wanted time to think. Mr. Azopardi's offer had come at exactly the right time. Her mother was in Belleville; things were unsettled with Ross; her job was beginning to bore her. There was nothing to keep her in Paris. But, although she'd been quite happy on her own in England, Laura was still unsure. After all, when she'd been in England she had still had a family in Paris to come home to. And her mother relied on her more since she'd been widowed. Laura wondered, too, how she would like living in New York. Before she had time to formulate any questions, however, Leonardo interrupted her thoughts.

"Your salary there will be a lot more than what I can possibly pay you here," he said. And, to make the whole idea irresistible to Laura, he mentioned the figure. It took Laura a second to translate the sum into French francs.

"But that's incredible. I don't even earn half of that here."

"And you don't have to worry about where you'll live—the job comes with an apartment, all furnished." Leonardo was encouraged by Laura's awed smile. "Mr.

Azopardi wants to talk all this over with you, of course. If you want to discuss anything with him, he'll be at the Claridge Hotel tomorrow morning at ten. Room 12. You can talk to him, ask him any questions you might have, and look over the contract."

"I'll go talk to him," Laura decided.

Leonardo was not surprised by her decision. After all, the offer was too good to refuse. He almost wished he'd been made such an offer himself—but then, he'd receive a fair profit if Laura went to work for Mr. Azopardi. He had never heard of such a windfall. These Americans didn't wait around when they decided to go after something, and he would encourage Laura to take advantage of it. *Business is business*, Leonardo thought with an avaricious smile.

Laura was still sitting there, lost in thought. When she had wished for something to break the routine, she had not expected such an overwhelming change to be offered to her. She was having trouble believing that any of this was really happening. And she would have to think of something to tell her mother. If Laura talked to her now, before seeing Mr. Azopardi, Mrs. Dolan would try to talk her out of going. Laura would have to present it as a fait accompli; she knew her mother would worry about her. But she'd been living on her own for a few years now, and she'd have to convince her mother that she could look after herself. She'd talk to Mr. Azopardi tomorrow, then make a trip to Belleville to explain things.

Laura realized that, as she'd been thinking, her mind was made up. No matter what Mr. Azopardi said, she would accept his offer. The only remaining problem was Ross. He would argue—it would be the same argument they had every time either of them made an independent decision.

Perhaps this job offer was the excuse she'd been looking for, Laura thought. Things would have to be resolved with Ross—and there was no sense in putting off that resolution. Maybe this trip to New York would force him to see things her way. He would realize that she really *was* ambitious and motivated. Besides, if he wanted to see her he could come to New York. It was only a few hours between New York and Paris, now that the Concorde was flying. *I'll take the job*, Laura decided.

But as the day wore on and the first wave of excitement wore off, she began to have doubts again. She wanted to discuss the whole thing with someone—Ross. He was the closest she could get to an objective third party; and besides, despite her job in London and her time spent at Leonardo's, Laura knew that Ross had more business sense than she did. He knew how big companies worked, and he had an idea of what life would be like in New York from his visit there a few years ago. He might be able to give her some idea of typical American salaries, or of what an American company might expect of her.

Each time the phone rang her spirits rose. But after several disappointments Laura began to worry. It wasn't like Ross not to call—she had always relied on him to patch up their quarrels. Normally her pride kept her from making the first move, but she needed his advice. Swallowing her pride, she called his office. A neutral voice informed her that Mr. Montclair was out;

that was all the recalcitrant secretary would say. Laura left the shop that afternoon feeling forlorn. Even the thought of her upcoming interview with Mr. Azopardi was depressing. She badly needed Ross's advice.

Isolated from him, Laura's imagination began to work feverishly. Was he plotting to keep her at arm's length? Was this his revenge for their silly argument? She could hardly believe that Ross was capable of such childish behavior. Laura paced back and forth in the tiny living room of her apartment, trying desperately to decide what to do. Without Ross's rational, calming influence, she felt off balance. She thought of turning to Sonia, asking her opinion, but something prevented her. She liked her roommate well enough, and they got along all right. But, deep down, Laura didn't trust her. She sometimes thought that Sonia found Ross attractive, and it worried her. She would have to think this through on her own. She relented enough to ask if there had been any calls for her. Sonia looked at her strangely, but said the phone hadn't rung. Laura held her tongue and continued her pacing. *I'll sleep on it*, she thought, *and make a decision in the morning.*

THE INTERVIEW WENT even better than Laura had hoped. She'd worried about it all night. Would Mr. Azopardi like her? Would the offer still be open? Were her qualifications good enough? She had worried needlessly; Leonardo had been right. The American company wanted her, and they wanted her to make up her mind right away. Mr. Azopardi briefly discussed the contract with her, mentioned the salary and the apartment, and then asked about her passport. He listed all the things she'd need to get—a vaccination, a visa, working papers—and then told her to be ready to sail on Saturday.

"Saturday? In four days? But I haven't given my notice to Leonardo! And my roommate doesn't know I'm leaving . . . and I have to say goodbye to my mother and . . . ."

Mr. Azopardi waited until Laura's objections ran out. "Well?" he asked her. "Do you want more time to think?" At Laura's nod he said, "I'll give you until tomorrow evening to make up your mind. If you decide to take the job come here and sign the contract."

Laura, her mind in a daze, could only nod her agreement. She left the hotel and walked home, too overwhelmed to think clearly.

Wednesday went by all too quickly. By four o'clock Laura had called Ross's office seven times. Each time, the same receptionist blandly informed her that Mr. Montclair was out. Laura couldn't get anything else out of the woman and finally gave up in frustration.

At five she left the office, still unsure of what to do. She walked aimlessly, trying to sort out her thoughts. The longer she walked, the angrier she became with Ross. Who did he think he was, to disappear like this when she needed him most? His selfishness was unbelievable! She became determined to show Ross that she could be as independent as he was. She could make decisions on her own, forge her career, even begin a new life. Her steps became firmer, her path more direct. Almost without thinking, she was in front of the Claridge Hotel.

She went in, walked to room 12 and firmly knocked on the door.

THURSDAY WAS AN exhausting day. Laura ran all over Paris making arrangements for her trip, then caught an evening train to Belleville. She tried to calm her mother's fears about life in New York and promised to write faithfully. She stayed with her mother Thursday night, returning to Paris around eleven the next morning. She had a million things left to do and barely enough time to do them. Mr. Azopardi had reserved a cabin for her on the S. S. *La Reine,* explaining that he wanted her to arrive in New York feeling relaxed and ready for a new life-style. She was to sail Saturday, at noon, from Le Havre. She flew around getting shots, buying shoes and books, trying to make sense of her momentous decision.

But in between the bookshops and the shoe stores Laura tried one more time to call Ross. She was ready to forgive him and to ask his advice, but the phone rang and rang in the deserted apartment. Numbed, Laura hung up. Then she began to get angry again.

He's out on the town while I'm suffering, she fumed. Anger and disappointment warred for possession of her heart. Rather than give in to her pain, Laura steeled herself and took refuge in her pride. She continued her preparations for her journey. Her heart wasn't in it, but she refused to listen to her heart. She'd be on the S. S. *La Reine* at noon the next day.

She didn't want Ross to worry about her, though—or worse, to think her decision had anything to do with him. She decided to leave him a note, explaining where she was. She also told him when her ship was leaving . . . just in case he relented, and wanted to see her off. She also told him which train she'd be on for Le Havre. He might even ride with her to Le Havre and keep her company until the boat lifted anchor. The train trip would give them time to make up and start thinking about the future.

The night was warm and Laura walked all the way to Ross's apartment. She dropped the note in his mailbox and felt relieved. She knew she could count on him . . . he'd get her note and meet her at the station. They'd have a few hours together, time to think and to plan. Laura looked forward happily to the next day, when she'd see Ross again. She walked home feeling at peace with the world.

AT THE MOMENT Laura's note slid into his mailbox, Ross was pacing the midnight streets of Brussels. He was beginning to regret his abrupt departure from Paris—and he missed Laura. Totally exhausted and feeling lonely, Ross decided to forget his pride. Once again, Laura's determination would outlast his—but this time he didn't mind. He would call her long-distance and apologize. It was too late to call that night but he had some free time the next day after lunch. He would call and surprise her. Feeling more cheerful, Ross made his way back to his hotel.

Chapter 3

A crowd of friends surrounded Laura. They swirled around her, calling back and forth, forming a solid obstruction on the platform at the Saint Lazare Station in Paris. They talked and teased and cajoled, but Laura was deaf to their words of encouragement. She wanted to see only one face, hear only one voice. She searched for Ross in the crowd and was oblivious to everyone else. The fond farewells and compliments had a hollow ring without Ross to share them. As the minutes passed she began to panic. She was on the point of trying his number one last time, but then she realized that if Ross wanted to see her he would be at the station. As much as she wanted to see him, Laura wasn't willing to make a nuisance of herself. She knew everyone was commenting on his absence; she couldn't face talking to him, being rejected and trying to hold her head high in front of this crowd. She looked at a nearby pay phone . . . but her feet refused to move.

The door slammed shut and the train began to pull slowly out of the station. Laura stayed glued to the window, hoping against hope that Ross would come racing alongside the train. But his handsome face didn't appear. *It only happens in the movies*, Laura thought. Dejectedly, she found her seat.

She cried almost all the way to Le Havre. Then she saw a ray of hope: perhaps Ross, wishing to avoid the crowd he would expect at the Saint Lazare station, had decided to see her off at the ship. Laura began to feel a little better and by the time she reached Le Havre she was eagerly watching for a glimpse of Ross's face. She didn't see him from the train or in the station, and he wasn't waiting for her at the S. S. *La Reine.*

Refusing to give up all hope, Laura waited on the dock until the last minute. The ship's siren sounded its last call, and to Laura's ears it was a funeral dirge. She walked forlornly up the gangplank just as it was being lifted. As the grand, oceangoing vessel moved into the Channel, she felt as if the only important bond linking her with her homeland was disappearing. Gone was the security of life with Ross; isolation and regret had come to replace it.

The first few moments of her cruise to America passed, for Laura, in ineffable sadness. She wanted to turn back the clock, to go back to the happy, carefree days of her childhood, when Ross had been her best friend and her world was secure. And she realized that things had never been bad between them, just badly timed . . . until this past week. Laura examined her behavior, and knew she could have been more gentle with Ross, more generous. She regretted her impulsive actions and decisions, and vowed to write to him from the ship.

Lost in her reverie, she had been unaware of the ship's motion. Now she looked up and saw nothing but water. She had left France behind. Laura vowed to try to leave her sense of loss behind, as well. She was on a luxury liner, surrounded by opulence and wealth. Here was a new world, ready to charm away the pain of the past. Why should she refuse its spell?

There was a discreet knock at the cabin door and a stewardess appeared. "My name is Anna. Can I help you get settled?" Laura declined the offer politely, feeling she wasn't quite ready to confront the world yet.

Anna disappeared up the gangway, leaving Laura to unpack the things she would need on the ship. She put on a little makeup and changed her dress. Then, reassured by the image the mirror reflected, she felt ready to meet her fellow travelers. She went up on deck.

The other passengers were converging on the deck chairs. Laura looked around in confusion and just then a member of the staff with a clipboard came up to her.

"Have you reserved a chair?"

"I don't think so," Laura replied hesitantly.

"What's your name, please?"

Laura told him her name and the man searched his list. "You do have a chair," he concluded. "It was reserved at the same time as your ticket."

Still feeling a bit timid in her new world, Laura mentally thanked her considerate employers who'd thought of her every need. *Perhaps it's a good sign*, she thought, stretching out in the sun. The deck attendant went off to see to his other passengers after covering Laura's legs with a luxuriously thick wool blanket.

She soon lost herself in the gentle movement of the ship. *This is the life for me*, she thought lazily, *being pampered on an ocean cruise*. She began to enjoy herself and to look forward to her arrival in New York. She tried to imagine her new employers, the city itself, and her apartment. . . . Gradually Laura began to relax. Life would be all right, she was sure of it. After a few moments she rose from her chair and went to lean on the deck railing. She stared down at the hypnotizing pattern of the waves, but the cold breeze made her musings less than pleasant, and soon she gave up her place at the railing to seek shelter under the covered part of the deck.

As she walked along one of the passageways that led to the elevator, she noticed an unusual couple about to descend the stairway. The man was tall and thin and a little stooped. He looked old and fragile, and his dress reinforced the oddness of his appearance: he was shivering under a cape that made him look like a traveler from the nineteenth century. His worn face, dark, sunken eyes and haunted expression made Laura stop and stare as he came toward her, using a cane for support. His companion was wearing a nurse's uniform, but looked pretty in spite of her austere outfit. She held a plaid blanket in one hand, and with the other she guided her patient.

As they passed Laura in the passageway, the nurse raised her eyes quickly and caught Laura staring at them. Laura blushed and looked away, but the nurse didn't seem at all displeased. She smiled and nodded as if she were quite accustomed to being examined. Putting all thought of the encounter out of her mind, Laura went on to her cabin, where she sank into a peaceful sleep.

As it was their first day out, the head of protocol had invited several distinguished first-class passengers to a reception. Laura had been included—one more thoughtful gesture by Jenkins & Company, who'd let it be known that she represented one of the finest fashion houses in Paris. Laura looked forward to the occasion and dressed carefully for her first formal meeting with her fellow travelers. Thanks to her job, she had many fine, tasteful, long dresses from which to choose. She selected one that was elegant but conservative—a good image to present, she thought, not wanting to let Jenkins & Company down. When she felt ready and had her nerves to some extent under control, she went to the salon. As she walked in, she saw again the romantic-looking passenger she'd noticed in the passageway. He'd traded his cloak for an elegant tuxedo, but in his eyes was the same expression of suffering. Laura thought he looked as if he were in perpetual mourning. *A heartful of shadows,* she said to herself as the members of the exclusive circle were introduced to each other.

Laura listened carefully when the intriguing passenger was presented to the group. The head of protocol announced, with a hint of deference in his voice, "Mr. Sidney Collins."

The man held out his hand to Laura and a glimmer of interest seemed to flare in his dark eyes.

The ship's officer noticed Laura's blank face and was about to give her a few facts on the man he had just introduced her to. But before he had a chance to say more than the man's name he was interrupted. An enthusiastic lady on the other side of fifty burst out, "Everyone knows who Sidney is! He's a worldwide phenomenon!"

A chorus of female voices sang the praises of Mr. Collins and a swarm of women separated him from Laura. But Laura noticed that the celebrity in question didn't appear to appreciate the homage he was receiving. He swallowed his drink and took his leave as quickly as he could—as if he needed to escape the comments and admiring glances of his fellow travelers. But before he left the room his eyes came to rest, for a long moment, on Laura's face. Laura thought fleetingly of Zizi, and the younger woman's unshakable belief that every man who saw Laura fell head over heels in love with her. *Crazy Zizi*, Laura thought, and could almost hear the little fitter's conclusion: "You've got a knack, Laura!" Laura smiled to herself. She knew that there had been nothing warm or even intrigued about Mr. Collin's gaze; he had simply been seeking some piece of information from her face, she thought.

When the salon door closed behind the enigmatic passenger the room burst into a flurry of speculations. All the women were intrigued, and Laura heard the same comment over and over: how cruel fate had been.

She turned to a pleasant-looking gentleman with a military bearing. "Who is Sidney Collins?" she asked.

"Don't you know him? He's a famous American conductor and composer—he wrote *Eliana* and *Magaladi*. You've never heard of him?"

A glimmer of memory stirred in Laura's head. "I think I have," she said. "Now that you mention it, I do remember him. I've heard some of his records; they're excellent. But everyone seems to be pitying him. What happened?"

"It was a terrible tragedy. He was crazy about his wife—positively adored her—and he killed her."

"He *killed* her?"

"In an automobile accident. He had a really fast sports car and he always drove at top speed. One night, when she was in the car, he crashed into a light pole. She was killed instantly . . . and he just barely lived. It was during a European tour, near Lugano, I think, in Northern Italy. He's just gotten out of the hospital—in Switzerland. He was there for the better part of a year. Apparently the doctors worked like devils to patch him up, and it looks like they've succeeded, considering what they had to start with. But they say that his wife's death has really changed him. He doesn't want to see people, and he's given up music."

"He's stopped conducting? But maybe he'll change his mind."

"According to the papers, he's made his decision and that's that. He's quite rich, you know."

"So he can live without working?"

"So it seems."

"He still looks sick," Laura said thoughtfully, almost to herself. "Those hollow cheeks and sunken eyes . . . ."

"After the accident the doctors were pessimistic; they didn't think they could save him. But they've got him back on his feet again, even though they thought he'd be paralyzed for good."

"Poor man!" Laura echoed the pity of her traveling companions. "How old is he?"

"In his early forties. He was a respected conductor and a talented composer with a bright future. One bit of bad luck changed his life."

"You can never tell. Something might happen . . . he might become interested in life again."

"Let's hope so," her companion concluded.

He moved into the crowd, and Laura was left to herself. She had a glass of wine and chatted with several of the other passengers, but the reception exhausted her and she decided not to go to the dining room. Instead, she ordered a meal in her cabin and went to bed early. She didn't feel strong enough to face the exuberant crowds of passengers partying in every possible corner of the ship.

She tried to read for a while, but couldn't concentrate. As she waited for sleep to claim her, the somber face of Sidney Collins dominated her thoughts. His tragic eyes haunted her until she fell asleep.

LAURA WOKE UP on Sunday morning feeling refreshed and eager to find out what the new day would bring. Although the dining room was open, she didn't feel like eating yet. She put on warm slacks and a heavy sweater and went up on deck, reveling in the crisp, early-morning air and the rushing sound of the sparkling waves. She leaned on the railing and watched the waves, feeling contented and looking forward to the start of her new life.

By the time she had changed for breakfast, the first-class dining room was nearly full. A steward greeted her at the door, asked her name and directed her to her table. It was a table for four, beautifully laid, with a fresh daisy in a cut-glass vase at each place. Laura sat down and turned to the other person at the table, a middle-aged, pleasant-looking woman who introduced herself as Ruth Oliver and said she was an editor for a large American fashion magazine.

"We're in the same business," Laura said smiling. "I'm a fashion designer."

Mrs. Oliver laughed. "I'm afraid I take care of the recipe department."

Laura laughed, too, and decided she liked Mrs. Oliver. She had white hair and a face pink with powder, carefully applied to hide her wrinkles.

"I hope the crossing will be calm" she commented. "I get seasick easily."

"It doesn't seem to bother me," Laura answered.

The waiter came up to them and paused, ready to take their orders. As Laura turned to him to order her breakfast, Ruth interrupted pleasantly, "Oh, look! There are our illustrious fellow diners."

Laura turned to look, too, and saw Sidney Collins approaching with his pretty nurse by his side.

Mr. Collins said good morning to Laura and Ruth Oliver with the greatest respect, then introduced his nurse, Phyllis Baker. He then sat silently until his breakfast arrived, apparently oblivious to everyone else in the room. He ate with ferocious concentration, gracing Ruth's questions with one-syllable answers. Phyllis Baker's embarrassed smile seemed to ask forgiveness for her patient's difficult character.

As soon as he finished eating, Sidney Collins took his leave and his nurse followed in his footsteps. The atmosphere at the table was immediately calmer, and the other passengers in the room stopped glancing over curiously. Ruth and Laura relaxed and had a pleasant conversation over a second cup of coffee.

After breakfast Ruth wandered off to play shuffleboard and Laura took a brisk turn around the deck. Then, thinking it would be pleasant to sit in the sun and read, she went to the ship's library to select a light novel.

As she was browsing through the books, Phyllis Baker entered the library and sat in a cozy armchair with a sigh. She looked curiously at Laura but didn't speak. Finally Laura, attempting to break the ice, asked, "Is Mr. Collins resting?"

The nurse gave a tired nod. "I need a little rest myself. This job is absolutely exhausting."

"I can imagine. You have quite a responsibility."

"It's not that my boss is difficult to please," Phyllis went on, lighting a cigarette. "He's one of the nicest patients I've ever had to take care of. It's just that I can't leave his side. I'm afraid he won't take his pills or follow his treatments."

"Is he very sick?" Laura asked.

"He was. Because of the accident, nearly all his internal organs were affected—including his heart. He's only beginning to pull out of it now." She offered Laura her package of Camels. "Do you smoke?"

Laura nodded and Phyllis held out her lighter. For a moment, the two women smoked in silence, each absorbed by her own private thoughts.

"What do you say to getting a coffee upstairs?" Phyllis asked.

Laura was suspicious of the nurse's sudden friendliness. Although it seemed natural to make easy friendships on board the ship, where life was more casual than usual, it seemed to her that Phyllis's offer of companionship was not a casual one. She wondered uneasily if Phyllis had tracked her down in the library—after all, the nurse had made no friendly overtures to either Laura or Ruth at breakfast. Then she told herself she was being ridiculous—Miss Baker was probably just as bored as she was. The departure of the ocean liner had been exciting, but the rest of the trip would likely be sheer tedium, despite the staff's unending efforts to amuse the passengers.

A few people were playing cards in the informal dining room, and a chess set sat abandoned on one of the tables.

Phyllis glanced at it, and said, "That's the perfect thing for Mr. Collins. It's the only game that interests him."

"I like it, too," Laura said.

"Really? You play chess?"

"One of my friends taught me when I was young. I used to play a lot in England. I was pretty good at it once, but I haven't played for a few years."

"Would you be interested in playing a game or two with Mr. Collins? He has so little to do on board, and I know it would take his mind off his problems for a while."

"I don't know if I'd be such a good partner," Laura said hesitantly, trying not to commit herself to any routine. She wasn't sure she wanted to spend the rest of the crossing tied to a chessboard with a convalescing and taciturn stranger.

But Phyllis could be persuasive when she set her mind to it. Before she knew it, Laura had agreed to be in the games room at five o'clock—if Sidney could be persuaded to go along with the plan, as well.

Phyllis rushed off to try to cajole her employer into the chess game. Laura didn't know why, but she hoped Mr. Collins would decline the invitation. She stayed in the library, reading, until Phyllis returned. Mr. Collins had accepted the nurse's proposition.

AT EXACTLY FIVE O'CLOCK, Laura found herself seated in an armchair in front of a low table, face to face with Sidney Collins. Phyllis Baker had watched the two of them get settled, then she had disappeared. Sidney seemed to be reflecting endlessly on the best move for his pawn.

The game seemed to last forever. Neither spoke. Finally Sidney checkmated Laura's king and the game was over. He offered her a drink as a consolation prize, and they went up to the bar to unwind. Leaning back in his chair, and much more relaxed than she'd seen him,

Sidney seemed like a new man; for a few fleeting moments the look of a hunted beast was gone from his eyes. "You really remind me of someone," he told Laura.

Laura laughed, thinking of her trip to Nice and Zizi's zany stories. "I know. I've already been told I look like Delia Marston, the actress."

"I don't know Delia Marston."

"I don't, either. I wonder what she really looks like."

Sidney started to speak, then seemed to think better of it. Finally he said hesitantly, "You look like my wife."

Laura was taken aback. Not knowing what to say, she remained quiet. But, for some reason, the comparison made her feel distinctly uncomfortable.

"She's dead," Sidney Collins said abruptly. "Do you know about it?"

"N-no . . . I mean—"

"Everyone knows about it," he interrupted. "You might say it was a juicy bit of news. But for me, it was the end of life itself." Sidney had spoken quietly, and now he was lost in contemplation. He seemed completely comfortable in his isolation, but Laura felt excluded.

"You must have loved her," she ventured gently.

"More than my life. There was no one else like her . . . and there never will be. I might as well have died with her."

"I understand," Laura said softly. She was uncomfortable and embarrassed because she couldn't think of anything better to say. All words of consolation and courage had deserted her, and a heavy silence settled between them. Sidney turned away from her, offering her only his careworn profile and sagging shoulders.

Tears of sympathy filled Laura's eyes, perhaps because she saw the reflection of her own sorrow in

Sidney's situation. He turned and caught a glimpse of her face and saw tenderness and pain instead of the selfish curiosity he was accustomed to.

"I appreciate your sympathy," he said, then stood up, took hold of his cane and abruptly left the bar without looking back.

From that moment, a subtle bond began to form between the two passengers as their ship sailed serenely toward New York. Each afternoon they met for their chess game. And fate seemed to be smiling on them. Not only were they seated at the same table in the dining room, but their deck chairs were next to each other, as well.

"It looks like we're destined to meet up everywhere we go," Laura had remarked with a smile when she first saw Mr. Collins and his nurse take their places next to her. As time went by, she felt more and more at ease with him. And to Laura, there was nothing more gratifying than watching him emerge from his mournful isolation.

The days between Le Havre and New York passed quickly, strengthening their friendship. More than once, Laura caught a sad, distant look on Sidney's face, as if he were hoping to summon up the face of one who would never return. *I can't be that woman*, Laura thought at those times. *I can never take her place.*

"You're doing him a lot of good," Phyllis Baker told her. "You're the only woman who's been able to interest him at all. You're the first one to get him to emerge, even a little bit, from his isolation since the accident."

Just before the S. S. *La Reine* was to dock in New York, Sidney said to her in a strange, empty voice, "I suppose this is goodbye. I know I'll never forget you."

"The trip didn't last long enough," Laura answered,

trying to put as much of herself into her words as she could.

But their conversation ended there. Still, Phyllis insisted on giving her their address in Connecticut. "The house is only one hundred twenty miles from New York. Maybe you can come and see us one weekend."

"I don't know," Laura said, shaking her head. "I've got to get to work right away. I have a whole line of dresses to work on, and that won't leave much time for travel."

"That's too bad. The area's quite beautiful, and I know you'd like the house."

The nurse's invitation was scant compensation for Sidney's strange behavior; when the ship docked he took refuge in his cabin to avoid the crowds. But Laura had little time to feel hurt. After three steps on American soil she had to deal with customs, immigration and a routine—but incredibly thorough—search of her luggage. Then she had to arrange for the delivery of her trunk and other luggage. By the time she emerged into the packed, noisy streets of Manhattan, she'd practically forgotten her shipboard friends. She took several great gulps of air, trying to inhale the new country all at once. Then she began striding eagerly along the crowded, noisy sidewalk, heedless of her destination. She was free, alone, and in America! A whole new life was about to begin.

Chapter 4

With an expression of pure disbelief Laura stared at the uppity young civil servant at the French Consulate. "What do you mean a joke?" she asked.

"I'm afraid, miss," the man answered coolly, "that you've been the victim of a practical joker."

"A practical joker who was willing to pay for a first-class passage for me on the S. S. *La Reine* just for a laugh? That's not very likely!"

The civil servant shrugged and stole a glance at his watch. He didn't want to deal with this sophisticated but distraught young woman—and besides, he was late for his daily tennis game.

He burst out impatiently, "What do you want me to do? I've made an investigation and discovered that Jenkins & Company doesn't exist and never did exist—at least not as a clothing designer. Furthermore, design studios, especially haute couture, don't set up shop on Fifty-third Street."

"How could I know that?" Laura objected. "It's the first time I've been in New York."

Laura's voice was tinged with panic. *I shouldn't have come*, she thought. She'd been thinking exactly that for two days, and the panic had been growing steadily for those past forty-eight hours, beginning when her taxi dropped her off in front of the building on Fifty-third Street, and she discovered that Jenkins & Company, her new employers, simply did not exist.

She'd talked with the superintendent, with the fruit merchant next door and with the policeman who was directing traffic at the corner. The policeman was the most sympathetic, so she began explaining the whole situation. She'd told him she was French and had come to work at a company located at this address—a company that seemed to be nonexistent. The policeman listened patiently, trying to make sense of her story. "Go see your consulate," he advised her. "They'll know what to do."

By this time Laura was feeling totally bewildered. She was having trouble believing that any of this was really happening to her . . . it was a nightmare, and she couldn't cope with it. She listened carefully to the policeman, wrote down his directions to the consulate office and, in her heart, pinned all her hopes on her interview at the consulate. They would know what to do—even the policeman had said so.

After many wrong turns, Laura found her way to the Rockefeller Center. By the time she got there the panic had set in again, and she needed not only advice but some good, old-fashioned sympathy. She had always thought that the job of the consulate was to help travelers in difficulty, but the young man who'd been assigned to her case didn't seem to share her opinion. At first he flatly refused to believe her story. Once she convinced him that she was telling the truth, he reluctantly proceeded with an inquiry. The results were devastating: Jenkins & Company did not exist. Laura's contract was worthless. Her job and her apartment were chimeras, and existed only in her imagination—and Mr. Azopardi's. She had been deceived. . . . And the officious young clerk was ready to believe it was all a practical joke.

The strain was beginning to eat away at Laura's self-control. "But why would anyone do this? Why would anyone pay for my trip here just for a joke?" She took a deep breath and struggled to contain her panic. "What are you going to do?" she asked the clerk.

"I recommend that you file a charge. I'll take care of it. A charge against person or persons unknown, of course."

"Against the representative I spoke to in Paris?"

"You can start with him. Do you know him well?"

"Well, no . . . I only talked to him about this job in New York. But I know his name—it's Azopardi, Hermes Azopardi."

"Where did you meet him?"

"At the Claridge Hotel, in Paris."

"And you know nothing else about him? His exact line of work, his office address in Paris?"

Laura was beginning to feel very naive. "I only know he was representing Jenkins & Company," she said apologetically.

"A company that never existed. I think your Mr. Azopardi is about as real as the outfit he was working for. You signed a contract with a man who met you at a hotel and told you nothing about himself? Not very smart, Miss Dolan."

For Laura, it was the last straw. She didn't need an officious young civil servant telling her she had acted foolishly. "Well, what do you expect?" she burst out. "The buyer came to my employer's office and gave me the money to travel here—first-class, I might add!"

The young man raised his eyebrows in disbelief. "It *is* a strange story, there's no doubt about that. Why don't you call your boss and tell him what happened?"

"Can I call from here?" Laura asked.

"The switchboard will put you through; you can wait in the hall." He glanced at his watch again. "With the time difference, it'll be midmorning in Paris. If you phone right now, you might catch your boss before he leaves for lunch." Obviously happy to get rid of this troublesome girl, the clerk escorted her into the hallway and closed the door behind her.

Laura found the switchboard operator more sympathetic—and more cooperative. A minute later the telephone was ringing in the Paris office. Leonardo himself answered.

Laura was tempted to spill the details of the whole miserable adventure, but she thought better of it. Leonardo was hardly the soul of discretion, and he might be inclined to repeat everything to the other girls. Although she wanted sympathy, she refused to have everyone in the shop worrying about her. She was in a mess, it was true . . . but she'd have to muddle through it. An uproar in the Paris shop, no matter how sympathetic, would not help. She determined to keep the conversation as brief as possible.

"I have to get in touch with Hermes Azopardi—it's urgent," she told Leonardo in her most businesslike tone. "Do you have his address on his order forms?"

"He hasn't ordered anything!" Leonardo complained. "He looked at our lines, told me Jenkins & Company wanted to hire our designer, and since then I haven't seen hide nor hair of him. I'm still waiting for these orders of his to come flooding in. Why do you need to get in touch with him?"

"Doesn't he have an address in Paris?" Laura asked, ignoring Leonardo's question.

"Just the hotel address, where you went to see him."

"All right. Thank you, Leonardo."

He didn't have time to ask Laura what was behind her strange request; she'd already hung up. She thought for a moment, then asked the switchboard operator to call the Claridge. The information desk there informed her that Mr. Azopardi had spent a total of six days at the hotel and had left no forwarding address.

"But don't you have any records? Guests are usually requested to supply their home address, aren't they?"

"Just one moment, please."

To Laura the minutes seemed like hours; again she was pinning all her hopes on one thin thread. The Claridge Hotel was her last chance to get hold of Azopardi, the only man who could lead her out of this blind alley. The secretary's neutral voice came over the phone. "The gentleman in question resides in New York, at Jenkins & Company. It's on Fifty-third Street, number—"

"Thank you very much," Laura interrupted, dropping the receiver back onto the hook.

It was a dead end, pure and simple. Azopardi and his phantom company had folded up their tents and disappeared. Her contract was useless, not worth the paper it was printed on. One piece of the puzzle remained: why had a stranger paid her way across the Atlantic, only to leave her stranded on the streets of New York City?

Laura stood in the office of the consulate, trying desperately to make sense of the bizarre situation in which she found herself. But playing detective wasn't her prime concern. There was a more pressing matter: money. The hotel bill she was running up threatened her meager budget, and she wondered if she could hold out until the consulate came to her aid. Judging from the attitude of the unpleasant clerk, it would be some time before that happened.

Suddenly the enormity of her position burst in on Laura. She was stranded in a totally alien country, almost broke . . . and she knew no one but an ill-mannered young man in the consular office. She realized, in a panic, that she didn't even know his name. She ran back to his office. He was just leaving, his tennis racket tucked under his arm.

"Our offices close at four-thirty," he informed her in a curt voice.

"You have to help me . . . I don't know which way to turn! No one in Paris knows who this Mr. Azopardi is. It's crazy! It's like some kind of plot. I want to go back to France. I want you to send me home—right away."

"Send you home? Easier said than done! We need an order from the ambassador himself for that. After all, we have no idea if anything you're saying is true. It all sounds rather unlikely to me."

"What? How could you suspect me?"

"Listen, Miss Dolan," the tennis-playing undersecretary said impatiently, "every day all kinds of people come in here. They're all trying to extort a trip back home under one pretext or another. We can't send them all back without investigating each case individually."

"What can I do then?" Laura said, on the verge of tears. "I'm alone in this country. I don't know anyone. I don't know which way to turn."

"Don't you have any friends in New York?" he asked, a little more kindly.

"Nobody."

"You'll just have to stick it out at your hotel—do the best you can. It's Friday, and you can't do anything until after the weekend. See a movie or something, and come back Monday. Meanwhile, I'll let the consul know and we'll look at your case together."

"Couldn't I see him today and explain things to him?"

"The consul has left for the weekend, I'm afraid. I have to be going, too. I'll see you on Monday, Miss Dolan." And he disappeared into the elevator before Laura could say another word.

Laura couldn't bear to stand in the deserted hallway to wait for the elevator. After getting lost in the labyrinthine hallways of the Rockefeller Center, Laura found her way down the stairway into the street.

It was almost five o'clock, and the sidewalks were jammed with men and women escaping their offices for the weekend. She was carried along Fifth Avenue, pushed this way and that by an uncaring crowd, feeling totally discouraged. If the representatives of her own country wouldn't help her, who would? Her friends and family were thousands of miles away, totally unaware of the ordeal she was facing. Even if she called them and they could scrape together enough money to cover her passage home, the fare wouldn't reach her for at least three days. And besides, she would get everyone worried when they could do nothing. Laura thought achingly of Ross, but rejected the idea of calling him. She had gotten herself into this mess . . . she'd have to get herself out of it. She would wait until Monday to see what the consul could do for her.

She reached her hotel in a daze. The lobby was jammed with people who'd arrived for some convention, and their baggage literally made a mountain in the center of the lobby. They were full of coarse good humor, with their name tags and red blazers decorated with their company logo. The happy crowd increased Laura's sense of isolation. She headed straight for the elevator like a sleepwalker.

The anonymity of the hotel corridors confused her, and she wondered if she'd ever find her room. When she finally found it she opened the door, locked it behind her . . . and was overcome by the sense of desolation the austere room presented. It was, after all, just a hotel room, like a million other hotel rooms . . . it was as anonymous as the corridors had been, and offered neither a sense of comfort nor protection.

Laura crept onto the bed and cried. She hadn't cried so hard since her father died. She had felt then as she felt now—that she had lost all her security, that she was adrift in an unknown and unfamiliar world. Laura realized that, at the time of her father's death, she had hidden her loneliness with a mask of reason. And, after a time, she had regained her optimism.

But she hadn't done it alone . . . she had had protection. Ross's protection. Ross was her harbor, her armor against the world—and now she'd lost him. She had isolated herself from him completely—he might as well be a million miles away. Laura realized that, for all his patience, for all his tenderness, he had finally despaired of her. It was true that if he'd responded to her note she might never have made this trip—but she could hardly blame her predicament on him.

Suddenly Laura was determined to see this thing through on her own. She wouldn't call Ross and beg his help—she'd be strong and independent. She'd show him that she was capable, once and for all. She thought of the way he'd ignored her note, and her resolve was strengthened. *I needed him then*, she thought grimly, *and he didn't answer my plea. I won't ask him to help me again—especially not now. He's just like all the other men, living in a world of his own . . . wanting me to exist only when he needs me. Men! They're all the same!*

But were they all the same? As her mind wandered, touching on random images, Laura thought of another man. A tall, thin man whose features were worn by pain and remorse, whose eyes turned to the past, whose frowning mouth would brighten for her alone. . . .

Sidney Collins. Why hadn't she thought of him earlier? This strange, frightening country held at least one friend for her. She remembered Phyllis Baker's invitation: a weekend in Connecticut sounded like heaven at this point. And there was no point in sitting in her hotel room, waiting . . . waiting for help that might never come. Laura began to get excited at the prospect of a visit. Sidney had been all over the world—maybe he could even make some sense of the strange things that had happened to her. He wouldn't consider her a liar or a madwoman; he would be reassuring and comforting and . . . safe.

Laura searched feverishly through her wallet for the card Phyllis had pressed on her as they said their goodbyes on the dock. The card was her salvation, the telephone number a secret code, which would help her solve her dilemma.

"Silver Farm, West Cornwall, Connecticut," Laura murmured to herself as she dialed the number. "Please let there be someone home."

The hotel switchboard put her through. By the third ring, Laura was whispering feverishly, "Please . . . please . . . ."

Finally an impersonal male voice answered the phone and announced, "Silver Farm. Who's speaking, please?"

"I'm . . . I'm a friend of Mr. Collins. Could I speak to him?"

"One moment, please."

A few seconds went by. Phyllis Baker's efficient voice came on the line.

"This is Miss Baker speaking, Mr. Collins's nurse. Mr. Collins can't come to the phone right now. Can I help you?"

"Oh, Miss Baker, it's Laura Dolan." Overjoyed to hear a familiar voice, Laura cautioned herself not to appear too eager. "I would like to see you and I remembered you'd been nice enough to invite me for the weekend."

"Well, the invitation still holds, of course. How are you, Laura? And where are you?"

"In New York, at the Clarke Hotel."

Nothing seemed to trouble Miss Baker's efficient calm. She didn't question Laura's quick acceptance of her casual invitation—and for that, Laura was more than thankful. She was too distraught to try to explain her predicament over the phone.

"Do you have any way of getting here?" Phyllis inquired.

"I'm afraid not. I'm . . . I'm sort of at loose ends. I . . . I don't know a soul in New York."

"It was nice of you to think of spending a little of your time with us. Let me speak to Mr. Collins. Hold on a minute, all right?"

· And again Laura waited, her heart beating frantically. But already she felt better—Phyllis had calmed her, made her feel accepted. *It's true I'm being a bit forward*, she thought. *Phyllis might have invited me just to be polite.* The thought made her heart beat even faster. Then she realized that she would have called anyway—she didn't have any choice. She prayed that her behavior wouldn't be thought too aggressive.

But if the occupants of Silver Farm found her pushy, Sidney Collins certainly didn't let it show. His husky, warm voice was full of gratitude. "Nothing would please me more than to see you again. I'm looking forward to another good game of chess. When would you like to come? I'll send my chauffeur down."

Laura almost blurted, "Right away," but she stopped herself just in time. "Is tomorrow morning all right? I don't want to disturb your plans."

"Plans? What plans?" he asked, and Laura could hear a touch of bitterness in his voice. "I don't know what to do with myself. I'm already looking forward to having you here. Is nine o'clock all right? I'll make sure Frank is there by nine—Frank's my chauffeur."

"I'll be ready at nine on the dot. Thank you, Mr. Collins."

"I should be thanking you, Miss Dolan, for having

remembered a sad old man like myself. But I'll make
sure your stay isn't too unpleasant. See you tomorrow!"
And Sidney Collins hung up.

Slowly, Laura replaced the receiver. She took a deep
breath. She felt as if she'd been able to throw off a little
of the burden of confusion and isolation she'd been carrying since she set foot in America. A five-minute conversation with a man she'd scarcely met might not be
much, but for her it was more than enough. She had the
next day to look forward to, instead of the endless sense
of futility that had overwhelmed her. Her heart full of
hope, Laura slept.

Chapter 5

Silver Farm had been named after the groves of silver birches that bordered it on all sides. The house was built on the slope of a hill, and the rough terrain and dense woods surrounding it guaranteed its occupants total isolation from the rest of the world. It was an isolation that the master of the house was thankful for.

Sidney Collins had bought and restored the farm just after he had married Patricia. In those days his triumphant tours through the capitals of Europe let him spend without a second thought. He'd loved the Connecticut wilderness and the retreat it symbolized. It was peaceful and man had not intruded. On a nearby lake geese still settled each year on their seasonal migrations. In the early morning the fine, clear country light shone into Sidney's studio. It suited his hobby: he was a painter in his spare time. He set up his easel next to his grand piano, and a work in progress was always displayed. Painting had brought a moment of peace and profound satisfaction in the midst of the public successes of his vagabond life

But in the past six months Sidney had touched neither piano nor brushes. He didn't need to work to stay alive—he had inherited a fortune from his father, who owned some of the first offshore oil wells, and he had saved most of his own earnings. He would never be forced to practice his trade again . . . and he seemed to have no desire to do so.

He had fought his way out of a week-long coma in a Swiss hospital, but he had hit rock bottom in the process. He cared nothing for life. The house at Silver Farm, which had once sheltered so many happy memories, was like a prison cell. But on his release from the hospital he returned to Silver Farm . . . it was the only place he knew, and he wouldn't be bothered there . . . it was home. He knew he would convalesce . . . or die, and he was content to wait and see.

The doctors who had released him from the hospital were certain their famous patient was on the road to recovery. It was only a matter of time—they thought perhaps a year—before he could sit down once again at the piano and bewitch audiences with his emotion and technique.

The senior physician had made all this known to Phyllis Baker when she agreed to devote herself to Sidney Collins's recovery. "Healthy, calm surroundings combined with strict adherence to the treatment should lead to certain recovery. As for his present feeling of detachment and listlessness, it will fade away as Mr. Collins learns to live again. After all, he's still young. He'll leave this period of mourning behind and become interested in life again. That's what we're all hoping for, and I have no doubt that's exactly what will happen."

The chorus of medical men had added that they knew of several similar cases, and that the cures had been almost identical. The stronger the depression and despair, the more the patients loved life when time finally did heal their wounds. Armed with these predictions, Phyllis decided to stay by Sidney's side until his cure was complete.

SITTING COZILY in the rocking chair in his sitting room, Sidney Collins watched his nurse knitting. He seemed mesmerized by the ceaseless movement of her shiny steel needles, but his eyes were unfocused and his mind was obviously elsewhere. Phyllis had been working for him for six months, and by this time she'd become little more than a familiar piece of furniture. Her presence in the house at Silver Farm seemed to have no effect on him; he stubbornly remained in the world of his dreams, where he'd taken refuge from the pain and emptiness of his life.

Sidney glanced at the grandfather clock. Time had gained a new importance for him; he hadn't felt this way since the accident.

"When do you think they'll be here?"

"Around eleven o'clock, I would imagine," Phyllis answered without looking up.

"Did you notify Harriet?"

"About what?"

"The room . . . lunch . . . everything. I want everything to be in proper order when she gets here."

"Of course, sir. Don't worry—Harriet knows the routine."

"But she doesn't like to see new faces. I hope she ac-

cepts Laura's visit. It's because she worked for Patricia
before our marriage . . . she feels like it's her house, I
think."

Phyllis set down her knitting. "I'm sure Harriet will be
happy to see Miss Dolan. After all, she does bear a strik-
ing resemblance to your late wife."

"It's true, isn't it?" Sidney said quickly. "You noticed
it, as well."

"As much as I could tell, considering I never had the
honor of meeting Mrs. Collins—except through that
photograph." Phyllis glanced up at the rather formal
portrait Sidney displayed prominently on an end table.

"Patricia was even more beautiful than the
photograph," he said in a distant voice. "No other
woman is comparable."

He picked up the photograph and looked closely at
the face within the frame. His next words were spoken
more to that face than to his nurse. "When I first saw
Laura Dolan on that ship, I felt a shock travel through
me. She looked so much like Patricia. . . . The beautiful,
oval face . . . the curve of the mouth . . . the smile. Their
eyes are different, especially their expression. Pat's were
more gentle, more veiled; they didn't have Laura's forward, almost headstrong look. But Patricia's eyes . . . .
She was so beautiful. . . ."

"You mustn't talk like that, sir," Phyllis said in a
calm, even voice. "You'll get depressed again if you
don't calm down. Remember what the doctor said—"

"To hell with the doctor!" Sidney said, rising from his
chair and moving across the room with the help of his
cane.

"I hope the resemblance hasn't upset you too much."

"It didn't upset me . . . troubled is a better word." Collins was still, thinking. "It was so unexpected. For an instance I thought I was dreaming—that my mind was playing tricks on me. But then she spoke and the mirage vanished. I realized it wasn't Patricia. . . ."

He snapped his fingers. "It really doesn't matter. This uncanny resemblance between my wife and this young woman is just an accident of birth. It's the rest that counts: the personality, the charm, the character . . . the heart."

Collins fell silent, a gloomy, troubled look on his face. After a moment he began pacing again; the sound of his uneven footsteps was painful to hear.

"Is it bothering you that I invited Miss Dolan to visit us this weekend? After all, I gave her our address. I hope I haven't overstepped my boundaries," Phyllis said primly.

Collins halted and gave her a wry smile. "Not at all. You're being the perfect nurse, doing everything in your power to improve your patient's condition. In the six months you've been with me, you've earned nothing but praise."

"Thank you, sir," Phyllis said, evidently reassured. "I guess I was right in thinking Miss Dolan would help the time pass more quickly."

"She did. I dreaded that crossing. But it was a lot less painful than I thought it would be . . . thanks to her."

He limped over to the game table, where the ivory pawns from a fine old chess set were spread out. "And besides, she's a good chess player."

Just then the sound of a car's engine broke the silence. "There they are," Phyllis announced, "right on schedule. And it's also time for your medicine. Even though you have a guest, you have to follow the doctor's orders."

She stook up and went over to a beautiful, carved mahogany desk. She opened the drawer and removed a key, then unlocked a glass case built into one of the pigeonholes in the desk. She extracted a small blue bottle and carefully shook out two tiny tablets. Replacing the bottle, she relocked the case and replaced the key, then poured a glass of water from a decanter on the large pine table.

Meanwhile Sidney had pulled the curtain aside and was watching Laura get out of the car. He took the water and the tablets his nurse offered him and, placing the tablets in his mouth, drained the glass in one gulp.

"For once Frank stepped on it," he said. "And Miss Dolan must have been punctual, too. Show her in, Miss Baker. I'm just going in to put my jacket on."

HER TEARS FLOWING, Laura told Phyllis everything that had happened to her since she had arrived in New York. The details sounded so bizarre that even the unflappable Phyllis momentarily lost a little of her impassive exterior.

"It's even stranger than you think," Laura said. "That awful man who made me sign the contract doesn't even exist!"

"He doesn't exist?"

Laura described the phone calls she had made from the offices of the French Consulate. Hermes Azopardi had turned out to be untraceable. She told Phyllis what she suspected: that no one of that name had ever existed in the first place.

"What are you going to do now?" Phyllis asked, her

sympathetic blue eyes trained on Laura's tear-stained face.

"The clerk said he'd help me file a charge. But the consulate isn't open until Monday and I can't do anything without their help. Then . . . oh, I don't know what I'll do."

Phyllis put her arm around Laura's shoulders and showed the younger woman to her room. It was a large, comfortable room with two bay windows that overlooked the green countryside.

"The first thing you have to do is rest," Phyllis advised. "I'll speak to Mr. Collins about this. As long as you're here, you'll be safe from any . . . outside interference, so don't worry. We're in the middle of nowhere; the nearest house is eight miles away. The wilderness is so thick the racoons come down from the forest in the middle of the night to dig around in Harriet's garbage cans."

Laura had to smile. "Who's Harriet?"

"She's the cook. She's been working for Mr. Collins since the beginning. She's from Kentucky, a little headstrong and too candid at times, but she has a heart of gold. You won't have to handle her moods—that's my job. Then there's Frank, the chauffeur, and that's the little world of Silver Farm." She patted Laura's shoulder maternally. "Try to enjoy yourself this weekend. On Monday you'll have to make some kind of decision, so you might as well rest up for it."

Encouraged by the nurse's concern and her comforting words, Laura washed her face and changed into a sweater and a pair of slacks she'd brought for her weekend in the country. Then, with Phyllis as guide, she went for a tour of Silver Farm.

The house had been built with local trees, like most of

the houses in the area. It was sturdy, and could stand up to the elements without sacrificing any of its beauty. Sidney had had a lot of work done on the house, and Laura loved the smell of the sycamore he had chosen for the interior trim. She toured the vast living room that overlooked a wooded valley, Sidney's workroom and a smaller room, which had been Patricia's favorite corner. Feeling a little like a trespasser, Laura stole a glance at Patricia's work table. On it were a few preliminary design sketches; the former mistress of the house had a taste for fabric, too.

A wide, terraced backyard held the promise of picnics, and an oak table had been placed on the terrace for just such occasions. Then Phyllis guided Laura through the kitchen, where an enormous woman wearing a gypsy scarf was busy working.

"Harriet, this is Laura Dolan, our weekend guest."

Harriet turned her back, grumbling, and headed toward the sink, where she began banging pots and pans under the pretext of washing them. Then she stared candidly at Laura.

"If I didn't know Miss Patricia didn't have a sister, I would have taken this girl for her," she said to Miss Baker.

"Miss Dolan does resemble the late Mrs. Collins a little."

Harriet glanced up at the ceiling. "He sees it, too?"

"Evidently."

Then Harriet gave Laura a hostile look and predicted, "It'll all come to no good. Far as I'm concerned, there could never be another Patricia here. You understand, miss?"

Laura smiled an embarrassed smile; she wasn't sure

she knew what Harriet was talking about. She didn't know whether the Kentucky drawl made the cook hard to understand, or if Harriet was being deliberately elliptical.

"What are you talking about?" Phyllis asked Harriet bluntly.

Harriet waved a finger in the air. "We'll see," she prophesied, then began banging the pots around again.

Phyllis and Laura left the cook to herself. Laura said hesitantly, "She looked angry. What was she talking about?"

Phyllis tapped her forehead. "I don't think she's playing with a full deck. She took Patricia's death very badly, and she has always blamed it on Mr. Collins. When we returned three days ago, she practically tore him to pieces, telling him he had no business being alive when his wife was in her grave. I don't need to tell you what kind of effect that had on him. I had to double his dose of sleeping pills."

"But she still wants to work for him?"

"She's used to the place . . . and the place is used to her. And, deep down, she really does care about Mr. Collins. She looks after him like a mother. The house would fall apart if it weren't for her. She's a little crazy, but a good cook all the same. And besides, it's not easy to get people to work out here in the middle of nowhere."

Chapter 6

Sidney Collins, Phyllis and Laura had lunch together in the wide, airy living room. Sidney seemed delighted to see Laura again, and made her feel welcome and comfortable. The food was excellent—Phyllis had been right about Harriet's cooking—and the atmosphere relaxing. As they ate, Phyllis briefly outlined to Sidney the misadventures their guest had been having in New York City. Sidney was the soul of sympathy. He seemed to be feeling much better than he had on the ship—he even smiled quite happily more than once. And his efforts to make Laura feel comfortable were unflagging.

Finally Sidney said, with a slight hesitation in his speech, "Miss Dolan, I very much want you to be at ease here and not think of your recent difficulties. You can stay at Silver Farm as long as you like, for as much time as you need to untangle this affair and make the necessary decisions. Simply make yourself at home."

Laura was touched. Sidney's offer would alleviate her financial problems—she was running out of money very quickly—but she could hardly just move in here and wait until the consulate solved all her problems for her.

She hesitated, but Phyllis was quick to encourage her to accept the offer. After all, Phyllis explained, her patient would benefit from a fresh face in the house. And generosity wasn't offered just to be refused.

"Stay a few days," she proposed, "and give yourself time to think things over. The mail and the telephone will give you all the contact you need with the rest of the world. What could you accomplish if you were in New York?"

Laura remembered the loneliness of her New York hotel room . . . a room she had trouble paying for. She remembered the crowds on the city sidewalks . . . millions of faces, none of them named, none of them familiar. She decided to stay on at Silver Farm. Her things were sent from New York; she settled into her life in Connecticut with no trouble, and the household seemed to accept her presence.

Her life quickly settled into a routine. There were small events to mark the passage of each day—meals were eaten, medication was given by the nurse to her patient at the scheduled times. The evening meal became a sort of ritual. Sidney, Phyllis and Laura would sit, as they had on Laura's first day at the farm, and talk as they ate. Laura soon found herself forgetting her two days of loneliness and panic in New York City.

She also realized that Sidney was much more sociable at home than he had been when she first met him on the S. S. *La Reine*. He was delighted to show off the countryside around his house. With Frank at the wheel, he and Laura would tour the small towns and charming, tree-lined roads of rural Connecticut.

And both of them enjoyed their endless chess games. As they had on the S. S. *La Reine*, they had a regular time for their games. Each day Laura found herself comfortably ensconced in an armchair, a cup of tea at her side, pondering Sidney's beautiful chessboard.

In the heat of the day they ventured out into the terraced backyard, where spring was bursting in glorious color and lush, green smells. They were joined by tame squirrels who came to eat nuts out of their hands with tiny, nervous gestures that thoroughly charmed Laura.

"Patricia trained them to do that. She loved the animals that lived around Silver Farm."

Sometimes, in the midst of Sidney's memories, a shadow would cross his face and the burden of his gloom would weigh down upon him. But unlike Miss Baker, who said she was following the doctors' advice, Laura didn't discourage him from talking about his beloved Patricia. She realized that Sidney still needed to live with Patricia's memory, and that evoking his past joys gave him a kind of bitter comfort. And she thought it was good for him to talk, rather than sit in morose silence.

Little by little, a clear picture of Patricia began to emerge. She became a third party in all their discussions, as if she were sitting there on a chair between them. Laura began to think of her as an absent companion, and her intrusions caused Laura no jealousy.

The one thing Sidney refused to discuss was his art. Valiantly, thinking it would do him good, Laura would launch into a discussion of music, painting or even his past successes. He would always cut her off.

"All that's over," he would interrupt her harshly. "I've retired."

"Retired? At forty-two?"

"No age is too young for despair."

But despite his pessimistic declarations, it was ob-

vious his spirits were improving. He began to leaf
through magazines and on one rare occasion Laura
heard him laugh.

"It's working beautifully," Phyllis congratulated her
during one of their talks.

The days and weeks went by. And Laura had her own
business to attend to. She wrote to her mother but
neglected to fill her in on all the details of her misadven-
ture in America. Mrs. Dolan had managed to save a little money, but not nearly enough to rescue Laura. There
was no use alarming her with a story, the outcome of
which was still uncertain.

Laura resolved to write to her former employer and
tell him everything that had transpired; after all, he had
a right to know. She managed to describe her predicament with plenty of humor, as if it were all a joke she
had decided to make the best of. Carefully, in spite of
the nonchalant tone of the letter, she requested her old
position in the company. She was sure Leonardo would
jump at the chance.

His answer came as a shock:

Your story is incredible—if that's the word for it—a
practical joke that must have cost the prankster a
pretty penny. But you're right to take it all in
stride; at least you got a free ride out of it. I knew
you'd land on your feet! Try to have a profitable
stay in America, from all points of view. When you
decide it's time to come home you can always have
your job back at the studio—that is, if the big salaries in America haven't spoiled you. Remember to
let me know one season ahead of time, because I've
hired someone to take your place and I can't break
her contract without notice. Besides, business

hasn't been good lately. Anyway, I won't bore you
with my troubles. . . .

Concealed in Leonardo's chatter was a clear message:
don't bother coming back now. Laura began to despair
again. Then she noticed that there was a note from Zizi
stuck in the envelope from Leonardo. Laura read it
eagerly.

I'm positively scandalized by your former roommate's behavior. Sonia has been seen everywhere
with Ross. His little red Austin is waiting for her
after work every day, just like in the days when
you were here. . . .

Stunned, Laura replaced both letters in the envelope.
She set the envelope carefully on the table, as if it contained a bomb. She took a deep breath and sat back, images of Ross floating through her mind. Ross and
Sonia . . . Ross and Sonia . . . . She wondered if Zizi
could have made a mistake—but Zizi would never have
written unless she was sure. Suddenly Laura was determined to shake off the torpor that had descended on her
since she'd decided to stay at Silver Farm. She'd been
here four weeks now, relaxing, accepting the generosity
of an invalid. She had been a guest far too long. Zizi's
news about Ross had reawakened Laura's fighting
spirit—she had things to do, decisions to make. She
could count on no one but herself.

She went in search of Phyllis and told her she was
planning to go to New York and look for work.

"Do you have enough money to get along for the first
week?" the nurse asked.

Laura was forced to admit that her pockets were empty. "But I'll do anything," she declared, ready to fight to stay alive. "Waitress, salesgirl, barmaid—it doesn't matter to me."

"But you don't have the right to work here."

"Why not? I have my contract, and papers to go with it."

"Your contract isn't worth a thing, and your papers entitle you to work for Jenkins & Company—no one else. You could get into big trouble with the immigration authorities."

Phyllis's reasoning knocked the wind out of Laura's sails. "Well, at the very worst they could deport me . . . send me back to France."

But to be ordered out of the country like a common criminal was more than she could bear. The idea of arriving in Paris escorted by two burly policemen was not amusing. But getting a job was still worth a try. She began packing her suitcase while Phyllis stood in the doorway watching.

"Why don't you ask Mr. Collins to help you out?" she suggested. "You know he likes you, and he's grateful for the time you've spent with him this past month. We both know you've done him a lot of good—he's less nervous, less depressed, and he's sleeping better. Even the doctor has noticed it. We can't help but feel grateful to you—both of us."

"It's very kind of you to give me the credit for his improvement. I've been noticing it, too. But even if I have contributed a bit to it, that still doesn't mean I should wear out my welcome. After all, I'm still a stranger, and Mr. Collins has already been more than generous. I can't ask any more of him."

"But you're not a stranger. I have the feeling he's beginning to see you as a true friend. And he doesn't have many friends, believe me. Since I've been working for him, I've watched him push everyone away, even people he's known for years. Yet he's welcomed you . . . perhaps because you remind him of his wife."

"But I can't take advantage of that resemblance."

"You have too many scruples. What's a few hundred dollars to him? What does he care about a ticket back to France? He's got money coming out of his ears," Phyllis said almost cynically.

Something in the nurse's tone made Laura hesitate. Perhaps she could ask Sidney's help. "If . . . do you think he could help me get a work permit through one of his contacts? I . . . I couldn't accept a ticket. Right now, the last thing I want to do is go back to France."

"Do you want me to speak to him about it?"

"Would you? He might not listen to me . . . but if you asked him . . . . I feel so awkward, but I don't know what else to do."

Before Laura gathered the courage to look up bashfully, Phyllis had disappeared. The nurse returned a minute later and announced in an even voice, "Mr. Collins wants to speak with you."

Laura tried to read the nurse's expression, but Phyllis's face was a mask.

"Mr. Collins is waiting for you in his studio," Phyllis continued in the same toneless voice. Then she turned on her heel and left.

LAURA STOOD TIMIDLY outside the door to Sidney's study. Only a few moments had passed since Phyllis had delivered his message, but to Laura time seemed to have stopped dead. Her first impulse had been to collect her possessions and run from Silver Farm . . . but she couldn't move. So she sat, frightened and alone, until she gathered the courage to face the master of the house. Her feet had unwillingly carried her to the study door, but she was having trouble knocking on it. Her thoughts were arrested by the most lyrical rush of music she had ever heard. She stood, entranced, until there was a pause, then she knocked timidly on the door.

"Come in!"

She slipped into the room, feeling as if she was entering a sacred sanctuary. Sidney was at the piano, his hands fairly flying over the keys. The notes seemed to be the true outpouring of all the emotions he had kept so tightly bottled up for so many months.

"Sit down," the musician ordered without turning around.

She took a place on the low couch and listened as Sidney played a Bach fugue. The energy he exuded, and his obviously flawless technique, helped Laura understand the feeling that drove thousands to listen to him interpret the master composers of the past. The music seemed to spring from his delicate but incredibly strong hands, and when he played a piece, he made it his. His two hands possessed a life of their own as they moved over the keys, weaving a magical spell. Through the complex, changing rhythms, Laura felt she was meeting Sidney for the very first time.

The brilliant flood of notes ended almost abruptly, and Collins spun around on the stool. The music still resounded in the air, weaving its spell . . . and Laura realized that another spell had been broken. Sidney was no longer an irascible invalid, living in the world of the

past; he had become a man again, harsh and masterful,
full of willful impulses. Laura sat silent, awed by this
remarkable transformation. She knew she would need
all her courage to deal with this new creature; she steeled herself to fight the music's magic.

"You took your time getting here," the musician said
abruptly.

"I . . . I'm sorry. . . ."

"I have two things to propose to you," he interrupted,
in a firm voice she'd never heard from him before.

"But—"

"Don't interrupt. You can answer after I've made my
proposals. Understood?"

Laura nodded silently. She was unsure of herself in
the face of this new Sidney Collins. She had known only
how to respond to the uncaring, bitter invalid; now she
was confronted by a master, strong enough to com-
mand respect and obedience.

"I have two solutions to offer you. First: I could call
up an airline company or a shipping line, whichever you
prefer, and reserve a ticket for any destination in Europe
you like."

"But I couldn't—"

"Don't argue. You'll pay me back whenever it's convenient. The money doesn't matter. What do you think
about returning home?"

"I . . . I was hoping to stay a little longer. Do you
think . . . could I get a work permit?"

"It would be very difficult. And if you got it, you'd be
all alone in New York; anything could happen to you.
Are you so seduced by New York?"

Laura shook her head. "It's not that, it's just that I
don't want to go home . . . not yet."

He gave her a long look, but his dark face was an inscrutable mask. "Then there's another option. You can stay here."

"I could never do that." Laura spoke instantly, rejecting his second option without thought.

"Hear me out first!" Sidney's voice rang out and she bit her lip. She realized that this new Sidney would brook no opposition to his plans. He was determined to have his own way, and Laura wasn't sure how to respond to him. "Is there something about your life here that displeases you, Laura?" he asked a little ironically.

Laura took a deep breath. "I can't continue to live on your generosity, that's all. Don't misunderstand, I . . . I really love it here. But I'm used to working and . . . and paying my own way. I want to get a job—be self-sufficient and . . . and independent."

Sidney had his answer ready. "I understand and admire your desire for independence. But if you stayed, you would have a very definite job here at Silver Farm."

"What job? Playing chess?" Laura asked somewhat sarcastically. She wondered uneasily if Sidney did understand. He had never been in her shoes, never been forced to work to stay alive. And anyone as rich as he was had likely never been offered charity. She would have to be strong to convince him.

"There's a bit more to it than a few games of chess," Sidney responded dryly.

His caustic remark only increased Laura's resolve. *Let him tempt me with his generosity*, Laura thought. *I won't accept it.* Her thoughts must have been mirrored in her face, because Sidney's tone immediately became more gentle.

"Come now," he said, "we've started off on the wrong

foot. I want you to listen to me . . . forget about your pride for a few moments. Now then, you say you don't want to go back to France. You have no one waiting for you there?" He watched her face, then added, "Perhaps not waiting for you anymore?"

Laura looked him straight in the eye, not wanting to think about Ross. "That's right."

"Then nothing should keep you from considering my offer in a favorable light. I'm asking you to stay here as my friend and as mistress of the house. Laura, I want to marry you."

"But—"

"Let's get one thing straight," Sidney interrupted, effectively silencing her. "I'm not doing this out of gratitude. I never asked for your pity, and I like to think you never offered it. It's true, it wouldn't be a conventional marriage. But forget about my illness, my wealth—and your pride. I've been thinking about this idea for a while. I've made up my mind about you: you're a reasonable, intelligent person, and a sensitive one, as well. It's your sensitivity that has most intrigued me. You must be . . . how old are you?"

"Twenty-three."

"That's what I thought. I'll soon be forty-three. That's a big difference—almost twice your age—but I hope you'll learn to forgive it. You know I've been sick and . . . and a bit pessimistic about the future. All I cared about was Patricia, the past, and the life we had shared together. My fantasies made the time pass quickly for a while. I needed no company; I was content with my dreams. But I have to admit that since I've come back to Silver Farm, my solitude has weighed more heavily on me than it did before. Then you came along:

you were free and you seemed to enjoy my company. Laura, you're the only one I want near me, perhaps because you remind me of Patricia, perhaps because you know how to listen when I want to talk about her. If you marry me, nothing will change between us. You'll gain a new name and a new sense of security but I won't ask for anything else. Perhaps later . . . ."

Sidney's voice trailed off and Laura looked into his face, at his haunted eyes and hollow cheeks. She didn't dare speak.

"No one can tell what this life will bring," he went on gloomily. "But if you can't get used to me, or if someday you have . . . other aspirations, I'll let go, I promise you. But for now, I . . . I don't want you to leave. I need you, Laura. Stay with me."

Laura was speechless. *How strange this man is*, she thought. *One minute he's a tyrant, willful, imperious, and the next he's pleading with me. This must be my first ride on the wheel of fortune. I came here as a supplicant . . . and now favors are asked of me.*

"I . . . I don't know what to say," she said with a nervous smile. "It all seems so mad, so impossible."

"Why? Because I've said I'd give you back your freedom if you asked for it?" He put his hand gently on the grand piano. "Laura, you've restored my love of music. Please . . . stay and finish your work."

"To help you, keep you company, make you better . . . I could do all that. But marriage—I'm . . . I'm not prepared. Couldn't I stay here as your companion?"

"I don't need a paid companion. What I need, Laura, is a real friend."

Laura was moved by this simple statement of fact, and she began to consider his proposal. He wasn't hard to be with; she even admired him a little. And then the ambitious part of her stepped in: she could see all the material advantages of the marriage he offered. Little by little, the bargain began to look more appealing. Yet still Laura hesitated.

"Mr. Collins . . ." she began, groping for words.

"Don't call me Mr. Collins. My name is Sidney."

Laura smiled. "This is making my head spin, Sidney. It's so unexpected."

"You don't have to answer in the next ten seconds, Laura. As long as you agree to consider my offer, I'll be happy. Do you want to sleep on it tonight and give me your answer tomorrow?"

"Please."

"All right. And I'll let you off our chess game tonight. I want you to have all the time you need to think it over."

He stook up, signaling the end of their discussion. Laura held out her hand awkwardly.

"It's an honor to know you think of me this way, Mr. Col—I mean, Sidney."

"You'll have plenty of time to thank me! See you tomorrow."

"Good night."

As Laura climbed the stairs to her room, her head was spinning. She needed someone to help her think, an objective listener. She couldn't begin to sort out the whirlpool of ideas in her mind.

"YOU'D BE CRAZY to turn down a deal like that!" Phyllis burst out when Laura described the conversation to her. "You'll be rich, my dear, very rich. I hope you've taken that into account. You can't begin to imagine my patient's real wealth. He lives simply, it's true, but he can finance any whim he wants. I'm sure he'd be willing to share his fortune."

"He did say he'd take care of my future. But I'm not really interested in money . . . as long as I don't have to worry about it. The most appealing thing about his offer is that I'll be able to forget about my troubles for a while."

Laura sighed and went to the bay window that overlooked the wooded hillside. "Besides, Sidney won't be so hard to live with. And I've really started to love Silver Farm."

"Good," Phyllis said, satisfied with the turn of events. "I can start looking for another position—I have a strong feeling that simply by being here, you'll soon put our patient on the road to recovery."

Laura took Phyllis's hands in hers. "You've been a real help to me. I'm grateful to you."

A slight smile played at the nurse's lips. "Don't thank me. I was working for myself."

"For yourself? What do you mean?"

Phyllis's voice was still pleasant, but from a distance something ominous rang through. "I hope your influence on my former employer will move him to show me his gratitude in a material fashion."

"Oh, Phyllis, if it's up to me, you can have anything you like!"

"I'm sure it'll be up to you," Phyllis answered coolly. "Up to the future Mrs. Sidney Collins."

She burst out laughing, and Laura had no choice but to laugh along.

Chapter 7

"What do you think of my decision, Miss Baker?"

It was ten o'clock, the time Mr. Collins received his daily injection. The windows in the musician's room were open wide and a clear, fresh country breeze pulled at the curtains. It was the end of May; downtown New York would already be feeling the onset of the summer heat. But at Silver Farm the air was balmy. The birch trees were shivering with leaves and the wild violets were beginning to show in the woods.

Miss Baker looked up from the black leather satchel that contained her medical equipment. She reached into the bag and extracted a hypodermic needle, then directed her attention to her patient.

The perfect nurse, Sidney thought to himself. He appreciated her reserve; without it, having her under his roof day after day would have been intolerable.

"What decision do you mean, sir?" Phyllis Baker asked.

"The one about your friend, Miss Dolan."

"Miss Dolan is not my friend," Phyllis corrected him

in a neutral voice. "I met her at the same time you did, on the *La Reine.*"

"But it's at your invitation that she's here."

"I thought her company would come as a relief to you."

"And you weren't mistaken. But now I want to know what you think of my decision."

Miss Baker considered for a moment, then answered her employer's question in an even voice. "I think you've made the right decision. Miss Dolan will brighten up Silver Farm, and eventually she can assume my functions."

Sidney Collins looked disapproving at his nurse's words, but Phyllis Baker remained implacable. Her attention was absorbed by the hypodermic needle she was preparing.

"Your arm, sir."

Collins rolled up his sleeve. When the nurse plunged the needle into his skin he grimaced, though he actually felt no pain. He had a healthy and tenacious fear of needles, no matter how many injections Miss Baker administered.

"Did I hurt you?"

"Not at all. You're very skillful, Miss Baker."

"Thank you."

It was a ritual of theirs; the same words were exchanged every morning without the slightest variation. Miss Baker put the tools of her trade back into her black leather satchel and prepared to slip out of the room with her usual discretion. Before she had the chance to take her leave, Sidney ordered, "Stay a little longer."

He got up from his rocking chair and paced the room,

keeping the nurse waiting by the doorway, bag in hand.

"Do you think she'll accept?" he asked finally, after much pacing.

"Well, I would imagine that everything will be fine . . . unless she has other plans. . . ."

"She hasn't," Sidney answered, "I've already checked." He limped over to the window and stared out at the silver birches. His preoccupation gave him no rest: he stared unseeingly at the magnificent property visible from his study window. Miss Baker waited, always patient; finally Sidney turned and faced her.

"Don't you think she's too young for an old man like me? I'm . . . well, you know my health isn't that of an athlete."

"You're not an old man. If it weren't for the accident you'd still be active, in the prime of life. And even if your marriage does seem a bit . . . unbalanced, there are certain compensations. Miss Dolan is a young woman who has her head squarely on her shoulders. The only thing that might trouble her is the fear of falling back into hard times, especially after tasting the good life. I hope I haven't spoken too frankly, sir . . . but it's something you might think about."

"That will never happen," Sidney burst out, slamming the desk top with his fist. "I'll shelter her from want for the rest of her life. She'll be protected while I'm alive and she'll have all my fortune when I die."

"All of it? Do you realize—"

"Of course, I realize. She'll inherit it all—and it's plenty for anyone," Sidney said with a self-satisfied smile. "If Patricia and I had been lucky enough to have a child, things would be different. But that was our one sorrow in twelve years of incredible happiness. My property is mine to dispose of, and I choose to give it to the woman who is willing to put up with my sadness, black moods, poor health and unstable character."

A wry smile played at Phyllis's lips. "I don't think Miss Dolan sees you in such a grim light. The portrait you paint of yourself is too severe; it's not a sacrifice to share a roof with you."

"That might be true for you, Miss Baker, because your only goal has been to try to turn a painful wreck into a human being again. But for her it's different. She's young, lively . . . she could grant herself any future she'd like. Anyway, only time will tell. If she accepts my proposal, I'll want you to call my lawyer; there's no reason to delay. And now, could you tell Miss Dolan I'll see her in a half hour?"

"Very good, sir."

As impassive as a sphinx, Miss Baker turned, left the room and carefully shut the door behind her.

THREE WEEKS LATER, on the twenty-third of June, Sidney Collins and Laura Dolan were married quietly in a small village church in Vermont. The marriage took place well away from the prying eyes of indiscreet journalists and curious star followers. Privacy was the order of the day: there was no lavish reception, no announcements and only the minimum number of witnesses. Laura, not understanding Sidney's reclusive tendencies, wondered what this isolation was designed to hide and insisted on sending an announcement to her friends in Paris.

Sidney Collin's name was well-known in France, and Laura knew her announcement would cause a stir among her friends. She knew that some of them would be proud of her, some amused. But when she saw Ross

Montclair's name on the fine, white envelope, a wave of regret froze the pen in her hand. She was bidding farewell to her youth and to the tender illusions of her first and only love.

Her marriage to Sidney Collins had no connection to her strongest dreams and deepest impulses. She remembered with sadness those carefree days in Paris, when Ross's little red Austin was waiting for her each evening after work. She had been so sure of herself then, so certain of what would make her happy. . . .

That had been less than six months ago. And now she was living in America, not working . . . and married. True, it was a marriage of convenience . . . but somehow that only seemed to make things worse. The cynics wouldn't call it convenience—they'd say she married for money. Laura knew it wasn't true, but she still felt desolate. She was all grown up now, and a married woman, but she felt as if she'd lost something essential in the process.

Phyllis Baker had been quick to point out that there were compensations. Sidney wasn't only rich, he was a talented celebrity. Laura would make that talent live again. It was a noble project, and it might even be enough to make this strange, passionless marriage worthwhile.

So Silver Farm continued in its peaceful routine. Phyllis devoted her time to her patient. Laura and Sidney continued their placid lives, strolling around the estate and playing their regular evening game of chess. Only one room in the house was disturbed by the change: the kitchen. When Sidney Collins returned home with his bride, Harriet hit the roof. She was not brave enough to criticize his new bride to the master of the house, so Harriet vented her rage on the implacable Miss Baker.

"I'll resign, Miss Baker, I'll resign! My poor Patricia's place has been taken by some foreigner—a woman Mr. Collins didn't even know three months ago!"

"But Mr. Collins can't live alone forever," Phyllis pointed out, trying to reason with the wrathful Harriet. "She just happened to be in the right place at the right time. He could just as well have married someone else."

"Ah, but that woman took advantage of him—she knew she looked like Patricia. It's a shame, a crying shame, to take advantage of a sad and lonely man."

"Now, Harriet, calm down. Mr. Collins asked her to marry him. She didn't ask him . . . and it wasn't her idea."

"It wasn't her idea—that's what you think. That's the only thing she had on her mind when she came here. Didn't she call you and beg an invitation?"

"She called because she was alone in New York and didn't have a penny. Mr. Collins is a generous man and he wanted to help her. Don't worry, the new Mrs. Collins won't get in your way."

"The new Mrs. Collins! I won't have it! I'm quitting this very day!"

"Wait a while, Harriet," Phyllis insisted. "I'll soon be quitting myself. With his wife at his side, Mr. Collins won't need me anymore. Give this new arrangement a chance. If you still haven't changed your mind, you can hand in your resignation when I do. But for my sake, wait until then."

"No, thank you. I won't have that plotting woman giving me orders!"

"Calm down, Harriet. Nothing's going to change. I'll

pass Mr. Collins's instructions on to you as long as I'm here. You won't have to deal with Miss Dolan—I mean, Mrs. Collins."

Finally Harriet was placated. She agreed to stay at Silver Farm until Phyllis left—but not a moment longer. Phyllis left the kitchen satisfied with their bargain.

SHORTLY AFTER her marriage, Sidney took Laura to his bank in New York City and set up a personal account in her name. She was given every financial advantage, and nothing was withheld from her. She loved fine and beautiful things, and didn't hesitate to indulge her whims.

Sidney's generosity seemed endless. He discovered that his new wife loved to drive, so he took her to Boston, where an acquaintance of his had a sports-car dealership. Any car she desired would be hers, he said with an elegant sweep of his hand. Laura finally settled on a little white Triumph, a car she'd always dreamed of owning. Ross had taught her to drive on the narrow Paris streets, and now she could zip along the back roads of Connecticut to her heart's content.

Surrounded by her new possessions, her first weeks of married life at Silver Farm reminded Laura of a fairy tale. But when the glitter of her new acquisitions began to wear thin, she had the time to contemplate the awesome step she had taken. She realized that her marriage really was like something out of a fairy tale, in more ways than one: she had married Sidney, and now he expected her to live happily ever after. Their life was lived with almost impossible regularity, and Laura began to feel like a wind-up toy.

The only gratifying aspect of her marriage was Sidney's gradual return to normalcy—but even here she seemed to be losing ground. Her husband's moods ranged from melancholy to angry outbursts, and his breakthroughs, which used to instill hope in her, occurred only rarely now. Occasionally she would try to lure him to the piano bench, but he would push her away angrily. Sometimes he spent whole days locked in his room. Only Phyllis was admitted, to administer his routine medications.

Laura began to wonder why she had married this enigmatic man. As usual, she confided her doubts to Phyllis, and the nurse counseled patience. As she explained it, Sidney's shock had been so profound that a long, slow recovery period was only logical, and an occasional relapse natural. She thought that all Laura could do was wait.

And wait Laura did; she really had no choice. On rare occasions her patience was rewarded: Sidney sat at the piano, playing for her and her alone. As she listened she would tell herself that any period of suspense was worth this special reward.

But in spite of these rare moments of communion, she had to admit that the bonds linking her to her husband were indeed tenuous. Her husband . . . the phrase didn't seem to fit. When she thought of their precarious relationship, and the sterility of their life-style, she felt as if she were living in a doll's house that could be folded up and carried away at any moment.

Though she was officially the mistress of Silver Farm, Laura was a stranger in her own home. Her husband refused to let her change anything. Every detail of the house remained the same in memory of Patricia. Laura could do anything she wished in her own room, but the rest of the house was sacrosanct.

Even the day-to-day details of running the house were taken care of. Harriet adamantly refused her help in the kitchen, and Phyllis continued to take care of Sidney's medical needs. Within the house, Laura led an empty life.

Outside Silver Farm things were no better. Laura's new husband had no friends, and he had no desire to make any. Laura herself knew no one, and was denied the privilege of meeting new people. Besides the occasional tradesman, Silver Farm's only visitor was Dr. Burkes, an extremely busy young man who rushed in from West Cornwall once a week. He dealt solely with Phyllis and her patient, although he had deigned to congratulate Laura on her marriage and to express his hope that her companionship would facilitate his famous patient's recovery. Beneath his hastily pronounced niceties Laura detected surprise and distrust, as if the doctor suspected her motives. It was enough to keep the two of them at arm's length.

So Laura's contacts were limited to the staff at Silver Farm. Frank, the chauffeur, a village girl who came in to help Harriet and Billy, the gardener, made up her circle of friends. When she agreed to marry Sidney, she knew the life she was about to embark on would be far from normal . . . but she'd been hoping for a little more than this.

Sometimes Laura would wake up in the middle of the night, gasping for breath and trying desperately to remember where she was. Slowly she would piece together her life since coming to America. Then she would think of her present situation . . . and her next thoughts were always of escape. She reviewed the events of the past few months slowly in her mind. *Why on earth did I ever agree to this marriage*, she wondered. She would get up, go to the window and watch the sun come up behind the silver birch trees.

Because Laura confided in her, Phyllis had no trouble sensing Laura was nearing the end of her rope.

"Why don't you take up gardening?" Phyllis asked her one day. "It would be *your* garden, yours alone. It's the one thing at Silver Farm Patricia was never interested in. You could do what you wanted there, without having to worry about treading on any sacred or cherished memories."

Laura soon transformed the garden into her own private domain. The rich earth, the plants and flowers gave her pleasure, though she knew deep inside they were a poor substitute for what her real role in the house should have been. She got along well with old Billy, the gardener, and he ordered her plants, seeds and anything she needed. The garden eased Laura's tensions a little, and her new hobby pleased her husband. When he watched her coming back to the house, her arms full of flowers, the gloom would leave his face for a moment, and he would look almost happy.

She worked on the garden through the rest of the summer, delighting in watching the ever changing panorama of blossoms. One morning, as she was arranging marigolds in a copper vase, Laura noticed her husband in front of his easel, his hands full of paints and brushes. Her heart leaped at the sight, and she eagerly told Phyllis about her discovery.

"If he's starting to paint again, maybe that means he's finally recovering," Laura remarked hopefully.

Phyllis agreed; she had also noticed an all-round improvement in her patient's state of mind. His depressions were less frequent, and his temperament less melancholy. It was as if he were slowly emerging from a deep abyss.

Phyllis and Laura weren't the only ones to notice it; Dr. Burkes said the same thing. Laura's presence and the inevitable passage of time were beginning to take effect. The only thing the doctor worried about was the severe winter weather; in his opinion, a somber Connecticut winter would affect his patient adversely. He suggested a season in Florida or Bermuda, and tactfully indicated that such a holiday had to be planned well in advance. Why not make the suggestion to Mr. Collins now, he prompted—after all, autumn was already approaching.

Laura was delighted at the prospect of escaping the monotony of Silver Farm, and she urged Sidney to agree. He reacted with his usual indifference.

"If that's your wish, then why not? We'll go spend a season in the sun."

Phyllis's reaction was equally phlegmatic. "Mr. Collins won't be needing my services anymore, so I won't accompany you. You can give him his injections and his medicine; there's nothing to it. I'll have the chance to take a vacation, and you'll learn how to do without me. And anyway, it would be nice for you and Mr. Collins to be alone together. Maybe you'll find the closeness you seem to be missing so much."

Laura was grateful for the nurse's calm acceptance of her plans—and for her understanding. With both his wife and his nurse working on him, Sidney soon accepted the idea of a trip to Florida. Laura was happy, working in the garden and planning their trip—at last, she had something to look forward to. But the pleasant atmosphere at Silver Farm was soon shattered. When Harriet heard about the proposed trip, she blew her stack and vented her volatile temper on her master's best china, then tendered her resignation.

"She can go to hell!" Sidney burst out when Phyllis informed him of the cook's latest escapade.

Harriet considered herself the foundation of the household at Silver Farms; it never occurred to her that her resignation would be accepted. When Phyllis, who was beginning to feel slightly harried, reported Sidney's reaction, Harriet went to her room to pack her suitcases. Two days before the Collins' trip to Florida, she left Silver Farm for good.

Phyllis planned to escort Harriet to the airport. Harriet's plane left on Thursday afternoon, so Harriet and Phyllis would start out Thursday morning with Frank at the wheel. They'd take Harriet to the airport, then Frank would drop Phyllis off in West Cornwall. Phyllis would have Thursday night off—she wanted to go to a movie—stay at the motel in West Cornwall, and Frank would bring her back to Silver Farm early Friday morning. She explained all this to Laura, then asked if the younger woman would mind giving Sidney his medicine.

"I'd be glad to. That way I can begin my new nursing job."

"Beth will be here all day while I'm away. She can stay here if you don't want to be alone," Phyllis suggested.

"I don't need anyone here. I'll watch TV if I feel like it, and go to sleep early myself," Laura answered.

Thursday passed pleasantly. Beth, a young village girl who had been helping Phyllis for a few weeks, stayed out of Laura's way. Laura worked in her garden all day. Then she and Sidney had had a quiet dinner.

As she lay in bed that night, Laura thought of Harriet's departure. She felt badly for the woman, who would be forced to look for a new job after working in one place for more than fifteen years. But Harriet's departure might be a blessing in disguise, Laura thought sleepily. The cook had been forever raising Patricia's ghost.

Perhaps, with Harriet's departure, Patricia's hold over Silver Farm would be broken. As the sleeping pill she had swallowed began to take effect, Laura thought happily of the day when she could begin to feel that she belonged to Silver Farm.

Chapter 8

Laura woke up with a start, desperately trying to remember where she was. A high-pitched scream had worked its way into her consciousness, which had been dulled by the sleeping pill she'd taken. The drug urged her to drift again into a chemical sleep. She was about to give into the urge when a second scream rang out. There were heavy footsteps and doors being slammed. She heard a man shouting. It was no nightmare; she was painfully awake.

Someone banged at her bedroom door. "Quick, Mrs. Collins, open up!"

It was Frank. Laura jumped out of bed, slipped on a bathrobe and opened the door.

"What's wrong?"

Frank's face was dead white. "Something . . . something terrible has happened."

He was gasping for breath and his panic began to overtake Laura. "What is it? What happened?" she demanded.

"Mr. Collins . . . ."

"What? What about Sidney?"

"He . . . he killed himself!"

Laura sat down on the bed, staring at Frank with a look of pure disbelief. Before she could form a coherent thought, Frank turned on his heel and ran down the hallway to the telephone. From the first floor came the echo of raised voices. Laura stood at the threshold of her bedroom, her hands crossed over her breast. Her room was safe; if she stepped out of it, something horrible would happen to her.

Then she shook off her paralysis and hurried down the hallway to Sidney's room, tying the belt around her bathrobe as she went. When she reached the door to Sidney's room she stopped abruptly, refusing to believe that what she saw was really there.

The early-morning sun was pouring into the room, making the wood gleam warmly. Sidney was stretched out on the bed, cold and rigid. His features seemed to have been sculpted in stone. Beth was on her knees in front of him, sobbing into a handkerchief.

Laura's poise and ability to cope deserted her. She stood staring for a moment, then burst into the room sobbing. She slowly approached the bed, mumbling under her breath, and was about to reach out to caress her husband's creased brow.

"Don't touch a thing!" The harsh order came from Phyllis. "The doctor will be coming shortly. I had Frank call him."

"The doctor? Do you think . . .?" Laura stared hopefully at Sidney's cold, marble face resting on the pillow.

"Don't worry," Phyllis said coolly. "He's quite dead."

Laura didn't question the nurse's strange, cold assurance. "I don't understand," she blurted out. "What . . . what . . . how did this happen?"

Phyllis pointed to the bedside table. "He swallowed the whole bottle of tablets."

"The whole bottle? But it was nearly full!"

"Exactly."

Laura could only stare numbly at the death mask of the man stretched out upon the bed. Her brain still refused to accept the fact that he was dead. She couldn't speak, couldn't ask any more questions. This was her husband, the man she had hoped to keep alive with her companionship and care. She looked up to meet the nurse's hard stare. Phyllis was observing her with a cool detachment. Her distant blue stare contained something hard and searching, something that set off warning bells in Laura's mind. Immediately the younger woman tried to collect her wits. Her self-preservation instincts were on the alert.

"Where did you find the bottle?" she asked guardedly.

"I picked it up by Mr. Collins's hand," Beth answered between her sobs. "The poor man dropped it before he died."

"But I put it away in the desk after giving him the correct dose. Right in the desk, where it always goes! I took out only one tablet, and brought a glass of water with it, just as you told me. Sidney seemed perfectly natural when I left him. He was in good spirits and ready to sleep."

"He must have changed his mind," Phyllis remarked dryly.

There was a false note in the nurse's level voice, and it alerted Laura's sixth sense. She searched Phyllis's face, trying in vain to penetrate the icy mask concealing the nurse's thoughts.

"You . . . you believe me, don't you?"

"What I believe hardly matters," came the cold, impersonal answer. "You can justify yourself to the doctor."

"Justify myself? Why should I justify myself? I did everything you told me to . . . I did everything just the way you do."

Just then Frank came back to the room. His face was still white, and he was breathless. "The doctor's on his way. He promised to hurry."

He glanced at the cold, still form lying on the bed, then at Laura and her pale, trembling features. His eyes contained only grief.

"Frank?" Laura said.

"Yes, Mrs. Collins?"

"Frank . . . what do you think really happened? Do you . . . have you thought about it?"

He didn't answer. He turned his grief-filled eyes from the bed to Laura . . . and then he cast a desperate glance in Phyllis's direction, like an actor who had forgotten his lines on stage.

"Go ahead and say what you think! Say it! Say it's all my fault!" Laura clenched her fists, staring wildly at her tormentors. All the tension of the past months had reached the boiling point, carrying her away in a flood of anger and frustration. "Answer me, you!"

"I never thought Mr. Collins would kill himself," Frank said slowly in a brooding voice.

His answer seemed to increase Laura's lack of control and once again she began to mutter under her breath, not looking at anyone else in the room. Finally she reached the breaking point. She threw herself onto the bed next to her husband and buried her face in the sheets, oblivious to everyone and everything in the room. Beth and Frank exchanged a hurried glance, a mixture of embarrassment and disapproval. A horn sounded outside.

"That must be the doctor. I'll let him in," Frank said, eager to escape the tension of the scene.

"I'll get it," Phyllis said sharply. "I have to talk to him."

Laura stifled her sobs. She, too, had heard the car horn. Through her tears she watched Phyllis's stiff form as the nurse hurried out of the room and an uncontrollable shiver swept through her.

As she lay there sobbing, Laura tried desperately to make sense of her husband's death. She combed the past, searching for some clue to Sidney's unexpected decision. Had he been in a darker mood than usual? Had Harriet's departure broken some spring in the delicate mechanism of his psyche? Perhaps the planned trip to Florida had undermined his self-confidence. Had his morbid desire to remain entrenched within the walls of Silver Farm been more than a whim? Perhaps the recluse had felt unable to cope with the real world. . . . But he had articulated none of this to his wife. He had hidden his intentions. He appeared so relaxed . . . and all the time he was formulating his dark plans, determined to put an end to his existence. But although his intentions had been concealed, his message was blindingly clear. Laura had brought no light into his life. Her presence had given him neither comfort nor hope. She was nothing more than a pale shadow of another woman . . . a woman he had obstinately kept by his side, a woman whose memory had been a sacred torture.

Overwhelmed by a sense of futility, Laura saw her life stretch ahead of her like a desert. She realized that all her efforts to bring happiness to those she loved had been pitifully feeble. And Sidney . . . she had given him the only things she had to give—solace, understanding, kindness. She had thought they were enough.

She thought about the previous night. It had been their first evening alone together at Silver Farm, and Laura had tried to make it special. She had arranged a dinner in Sidney's studio with wine and candlelight . . . and Sidney had talked to her.

"This is really pleasant," he had said. "You're so kind to me, but I'm afraid I don't do much for you."

Laura had protested, of course; it had become part of the pattern. He was a charming companion, intelligent, easy to talk to and talented, as well. At times like this, Laura enjoyed sharing a home with him.

"You ask for so little," he continued. "Patricia was more demanding . . . but I loved her."

Sidney's misery was painful to Laura, and she had tried to bring some light into her husband's life once again. "You know I could never take Patricia's place—and I'd never ask you to forget her, or to stop thinking about her. But you had a wonderful life together, you were happy. A love that was once joyful shouldn't be destructive. You allow it to devour everything: your work, your talents, your career. I can't be Patricia . . . but I could help you be happy, begin to live again. But I can't do it alone—I need your help. Is that too much to ask?"

Laura expected an angry outburst. She waited, but none came. Instead, he took her hands in his and said tenderly, "I am difficult to live with. I'm asking you to play an unnatural role; how can you be a wife to a man whose heart is absent?"

Laura searched for the right words, the words that might lift him from his sadness. But he clung to that sadness like a lifeline, and fed it with his fantasies. As she tried to formulate some words of hope Sidney added, "The worst part is that I really killed her."

"You're not responsible. It happened, Sidney, but it wasn't your fault. You must believe that."

Sidney shook his head. "If I hadn't been driving that day, she wouldn't have been killed."

"Then someone else would have been driving . . . maybe even Patricia. The same accident could have happened. You can't foresee such things, and you can't prevent them. You almost died, too . . . but you're alive. Can't you be happy about your own recovery?"

"Happy? No, I can't be happy. I wish I had died."

"Don't say that," Laura begged. "It's . . . it's selfish! And you have more than most people. You're a genius at the piano. You could give joy to so many others! And . . . and what about me? Don't I count at all for you?"

He gazed at her sadly, a little surprised by this sudden revolt from his quiet, helpful wife. Then a change came over his face. The bitter lines at the corners of his mouth faded away and he reached up and brushed away a stray wisp of hair from Laura's forehead.

"Really, you don't look like Patricia at all. It was a mirage, a passing illusion. Sometimes faces can be deceiving. . . ."

Laura held her breath, waiting for him to complete his thought. Then a smile appeared on his face.

"You deserve to be happy, Laura. You deserve more than I've been able to give you till now. Things will change one day, I promise you."

A light shone in his eyes, a light that held the promise of a better future. Laura had looked at her husband in the candlelight. His smile transformed his hollow face and Laura realized with a shock that—for the first time since she'd known him—her husband looked truly happy.

Chapter 9

Inspector Finch reread the report he had written on his investigation at Silver Farm. For the past three days he had been working hard, and had thought of little else but the Silver Farm case. The death of the musician had seemed suspicious to Finch from the start. It was nothing he could state objectively, but his professional instincts had been aroused by the circumstances of the death. He had had the body removed for an autopsy, and until the report came in he was learning all he could from the people involved. And the people he interviewed added to his feeling that something was wrong. Dr. Burkes, the deceased's personal physician, had stated his opinion unequivocally: his patient had vastly improved. It was unthinkable that Collins would take his own life. Burkes had felt strongly enough to order an inquest.

Finch had also spoken to Collins's nurse, and she had concurred with the doctor. Finch gave great credence to her opinion, because she had been treating Collins ever since he had been discharged from the Swiss hospital. According to the Baker woman, Sidney Collins had regained to some extent his love of life. He had gotten married, he was planning a trip to Florida. He had even reserved rooms in a Miami hotel and ordered his chauffeur to be ready the next morning. His bags were packed . . . and besides, he'd just ordered three new suits. Finch remembered the nurse's unhesitating question: does a man about to kill himself buy new clothes?

Inspector Finch brought his attention back to the efficient woman sitting in the armchair across from him, giving her opinions in a sensible tone of voice. Reasonable—that's the word he'd use to describe her. A little dry, perhaps, and a little reserved, but after all, she was a nurse. A nurse had to play the part. No makeup except for a hint of lipstick. Finch decided she must be pushing forty.

He glanced down at his notes on the desk. Phyllis Baker, nurse, age thirty-nine. A no-nonsense woman . . . a woman to be trusted.

"I'll reread your statement," Finch said calmly.

That was one of his old tricks, reading the statement of a witness out loud. Sometimes it made a person think twice when he heard his sworn testimony read in the detective's impassive voice.

Finch began reading in his dull monotone. " 'Frank Ripley, Mr. Collins's chauffeur, took me to the Boston airport to accompany Harriet Alvin, who was catching the four o'clock plane. It took off on time. We came back to West Cornwall and Mr. Ripley dropped me off at the St. James Motel. I'd reserved a room there because I wanted to take advantage of the trip and see a movie that night. I hadn't been to a movie in months. I brought Helen with me—she's Mr. Ripley's daughter. Frank picked us up after the movie and dropped me off at the motel. He met me there the next morning at seven o'clock—we wanted to be back to Silver Farm by eight. On the way we met up with Beth, the girl who's been helping me for the past few weeks. She lives halfway between Silver Farm and West Cornwall, and we decided to drive in a convoy of sort, since she has her own car. When we got to the house, I went inside first while Beth and Frank were parking their cars. When I got to the door, I had to wait for Beth anyway, since I hadn't brought my keys along and I didn't want to wake up Mrs. Collins, who usually sleeps late.

" 'Beth asked me if she could take up Mr. Collins's breakfast. I said that would be fine, and I helped her prepare it. Since we were ahead of schedule—it was a little before eight—we decided to have a cup of coffee first.' "

Inspector Finch raised his eyes from the page and gave Phyllis a searching look. "That *is* exactly what happened, isn't it?"

"Yes, sir."

"You have a nose for detail, Miss Baker. It's a rare quality in a witness." Then he went back to reading her statement in his plodding, methodical voice. " 'At eight o'clock, Beth and I went upstairs and I knocked at Mr. Collins's door. Since he didn't answer, I thought he was still sleeping and I asked Beth to come in with me. When Mr. Collins isn't awake, I usually ask her to take the tray back to the kitchen to keep the breakfast warm. The room was dark, so I went to open the curtains. Then I heard a crash followed immediately by a scream: Beth had dropped the tray. She was standing with one hand over her mouth and a finger pointing at the bed. I turned around and nearly screamed myself. Mr. Collins was lying half out of the bed, with his arms hanging almost to the floor. Just out of reach of his hand was an empty bottle. It was a terrible shock.'

"And you knew right away he was dead?" Finch asked Miss Baker, interrupting his own reading.

"My profession has taught me to recognize death. There was no doubt in my mind."

"So you went to his bedside and you found that Mr. Collins's forehead was cold?"

"The loss of body heat is one of the first indications of death."

"And you picked up the bottle. Meanwhile the chauffeur came running in after hearing the noise. He wanted to move the body. You stopped him. Why?"

"My patient's death seemed suspicious. You don't die suddenly at his age—unless there's some reason for it. I thought right away it might be an accident."

"And you blamed Mrs. Collins for it?"

"I'd trusted her with my patient just a few hours earlier. Except for his chronic depression, he was in perfect health. At first, I thought she'd been negligent—seeing the empty bottle at Mr. Collins's side gave me that idea. Beth and Frank agreed with me."

"They had the same thought you did?"

"Yes, as soon as they saw the bottle. They knew Mr. Collins took many kinds of pills and that an overdose of any of them could be dangerous."

"What did they say?"

"Beth was very upset. 'Why did Mrs. Collins leave that bottle lying around? Didn't she know there were enough pills to hurt him?' Frank was a little coarser. He said, 'She really did it this time! She must not have had her head screwed on straight!' "

"So you all blamed Mrs. Collins?"

"Put yourself in our place. Mr. Collins was our employer—and he treated us well. Silver Farm was a good place to work; we had a lot of independence."

"I see . . . and what did Frank and Beth think of Mrs. Collins?"

A muscle tightened in Miss Baker's face. "She'd only been here four months. They hadn't had time to make up their minds."

"And what did *you* think of her?"

"I hardly knew her. At the beginning I found her likable enough."

"At the beginning . . . right. And afterward?"

"Afterward . . . there were certain details I didn't like. But she seemed sincere enough."

"And now?"

"I would rather not say."

"I see."

Finch sorted through the papers on his desk and found the one he was looking for. He scanned the hastily written report. "Harriet . . . Alvin supplied a statement to my men as well. She's a lot less charitable than you about Mrs. Collins. She accuses the woman of plotting to marry Mr. Collins for his money. What do you think of that?"

"My only accusation is of negligence."

"Is it true, as Harriet Alvin contends, that Mrs. Collins begged an invitation to Silver Farm before her marriage?"

"A begged invitation? Not exactly. We met her on the ship. She reminded Mr. Collins of his deceased wife and he was more inclined than usual to be friendly. I encouraged their contact, I have to admit, since Miss

Dolan—she was Miss Dolan then—was bored by the
days at sea. Mr. Collins loved chess and it turned out
that she played the game, too. But their relationship
never went any further than that, and we said our goodbyes in New York. I gave her my address, as travelers
often do, without thinking twice about it. Mr. Collins
was so unsociable at the moment of parting that I
wanted to do something to make up for his rudeness.
Miss Dolan claimed to have a job in New York. Three
days later, she phoned."

"And did the speed of her call surprise you at all?"

"At the time, I believed her story, even though it
sounded quite complicated."

"And then later?'

"Later I was less inclined to believe it. But the truth of
her story hardly matters now. I'm just sorry I left my
patient in her care that night."

"Mrs. Alvin's opinion is that Mrs. Collins left the bottle near her husband on purpose. Do you suspect
anything of the kind?"

"I don't suspect anything. But there is one thing I
know for certain," Miss Baker declared. "Sidney Collins
didn't kill himself."

"Then what did he do?"

Phyllis looked directly into Finch's eyes with a hard,
impenetrable stare. For an instant they sized each other
up, the witness and the detective. Finally Phyllis said,
"The rest is your job. I've said all I can say."

"I see," Finch said again.

Miss Baker glanced around the living room, which
Finch had commandeered as an office. "Do you mind if I
leave Silver Farm? I have to start looking for another

job. I'm afraid I can't do without my salary for much longer."

Finch looked at her and masked his order in a polite request. "If you don't mind, I'd appreciate your staying around another two days until I wrap this up. I hope that's not too much to ask."

"Do you think two days are enough?"

"Enough for what?"

The nurse's voice was deadly cold. "Enough to find the guilty one," she said, then turned on her heel and left the room.

Finch stared morosely at the door Miss Baker had closed so firmly behind her. He was not at all happy about what was happening at Silver Farm . . . things were becoming more and more complicated. He got up and walked slowly to the bay window to admire the landscape, but even the garden had lost all semblance of tranquillity. Two policemen were stationed at the front door; two more were lighting up their cigarettes at the foot of the driveway. Inside the house itself, Finch's team of specialists was at work, poking around everywhere and getting underfoot. And in the background, Beth was doing her best to keep the house clean, stopping often to make pots of coffee for the policemen.

And there was the horde of reporters waiting at the gates of the property, ready to descend on Silver Farm like a plague of locusts. That was the worst part of it. Finch wasn't an ambitious man, and in the past three days he had wished often that Sidney Collins had died a hundred miles away, in some other district. True, Collins was an important man—some detectives would have given their right arm to work on a case as important as this one; it usually meant a promotion. But that was the last thing Finch was after. He had been hoping nothing would happen before his retirement—and now this. It was too much. All these reporters and all this publicity—it was the last thing he wanted.

Finch went back to his desk and sat down with a sigh. The reporters weren't his only problem—there was that poor French woman upstairs. She had been sitting in her room, terrified, for the past three days. She was so vulnerable. . . . Her life with Nurse Baker must have been tense at best. Baker made no bones about the fact that she considered the Collins woman guilty of criminal negligence, if not more. But Baker had been cooperative and helpful, answering the phone and in general holding the fort with true professional calm.

After the preliminary investigation Laura was asked politely, but very firmly, not to think of leaving Silver Farm until the autopsy had been completed.

"You can ask anyone you like to come visit you," Finch suggested. "A relative, a friend, whoever you think would help you the most."

"I don't have any friends," Laura answered in an expressionless voice. "No one. And I'm a long way from my country. I'm all alone."

Inspector Finch used to pride himself on his hard heart—but he was moved by the fear that showed in Laura's eyes. "All this'll be over soon enough," he reassured her. "I'm sorry we have to hold you here."

Despite what everyone said, Finch didn't believe she was guilty. It wasn't impossible that Collins would kill himself. The death of his first wife and the accident were enough to push anyone over the edge, especially a sensitive type. Another sleepless night, a moment of despair—all the elements were there. But Finch couldn't understand why Collins didn't try to shelter his wife from the blame that would inevitably fall on her.

Suicide, accident or murder . . . . It was the judge's job to decide. Finch was an inspector, and his role was to gather up the pieces. Someone else could fit them together.

Chapter 10

Laura was drifting, floating through something ugly, something unpleasant. She tried to slow down, to stop, so she could find out where she was. But each time she tried she would begin to suffocate; she would open her eyes and see only blackness. Frightened, she would begin to drift again. . . .

The knock on the door reached Laura through a dull, muffling fog. It was six o'clock in the evening; when she opened her eyes the room was full of shadows. After a few moments she pieced together who she was, where she was. Gradually her nightmare came back to her and she began to cry quietly. Three days of being caged in this tiny room had dulled her senses and stolen her precious fighting spirit.

She felt her way to the door and opened it. Two men stood there: Inspector Finch and a tall, harsh-looking man.

"The name's Hargest, from Hartford." The big man identified himself as he walked in, forcing Laura back into the room.

Finch came in after him with a contrite look on his

face. He pulled the door closed after him. "We have to talk to you, Mrs. Collins."

"Sit down," she said weakly.

The two men sat in armchairs by the window. Finch avoided Laura's eyes, but Hargest gave her a piercing look.

"We have the results of the autopsy," he announced.

"The autopsy?" she repeated, as if she didn't know the meaning of the word.

Finch put his hand on her arm and she nearly jumped. "Mrs. Collins, please, sit down."

She sat. She sat facing Hargest, looked him straight in the eye and began weeping quietly. Hargest, ignoring her tears, began speaking brusquely. Laura was making a last attempt to pull herself together when Hargest rapped out his first question.

"Do you order supplies for the garden?"

Laura stared at him and stopped crying. "Supplies?" she murmured, taken aback by the question.

"Yes, supplies," Hargest burst out. "Would you stop repeating everything I say? I'm here to ask the questions. You just answer them."

Laura stole a desperate glance at Finch, but he coughed into his hand and averted his eyes.

"Do you order the supplies for the garden?" Hargest demanded again. "Seeds, plants, trowels . . . garden supplies. Do you order them?"

"Yes . . . I've been taking care of the garden. Billy helps, but he's getting old and he doesn't take much initiative anymore."

Hargest smiled unpleasantly. "Initiative? Is that what you call it? Well, we'll see!"

He opened his briefcase and took out a folded, dog-eared piece of paper. He straightened it out on his knee while Finch stared off into space.

Running his finger down the list of articles described on the sheet, Hargest read them off under his breath. He found the one he was after and he looked up at Laura. "Did you order something called Herbex, a weed killer? Don't lie—I've got the bill here!"

"I don't see why I should lie," she shot back. "I already told you I order everything for the garden."

"Including Herbex?"

"Including Herbex, and everything else. I order from the catalogues and advertisements that are sent here. Billy suggested it—he said that's what most people around here do. Why do you find it strange?"

"Did you know Herbex is highly poisonous? Did you know its label contains the warning to keep it away from children and livestock?"

"There aren't any children at Silver Farm, and our livestock, as you call it, consists of stray racoons and squirrels. They occasionally get curious—that's why we keep everything locked up in the greenhouse."

"I asked you a question," Hargest barked in his harsh voice.

"What question? I've answered everything you asked me," Laura replied levelly. "What are you getting at?"

"I asked you whether you knew the product was poisonous!"

Laura stared at him. She couldn't follow his reasoning. Why was this chemical so important to him? She glanced at Finch but he avoided her eyes, refusing to help her.

"In the box of Herbex," Hargest went on, "there's a measuring spoon no bigger than a thimble. That tiny amount of chemical is meant to be dissolved in twelve quarts of water—and it's still enough to kill weeds and keep the ground infertile for months. Even a pinch of that powder would kill a human being. There were massive amounts of that powder in your husband's bloodstream, Mrs. Collins."

Laura stared. She opened her mouth to speak but Hargest cut her off.

"And that poison didn't enter his body all by itself, Mrs. Collins. He swallowed it—"

"No!"

"—in the glass of water *you* gave him!"

"No!" Every ounce of strength Laura possessed was concentrated in that one small word of denial. But Hargest wasn't listening.

"I accuse you of poisoning your husband, Mrs. Collins."

Again Laura uttered her one small word of denial. She stood up warily, searching Hargest's face. It was impassive; only the eyes contained expression, and they looked at her with loathing.

Shaken, Laura turned to Finch. He had been gentle with her before, and she thought she had detected sympathy in him even this evening, as Hargest questioned her. But Finch would not meet her eyes.

"You have to face facts," he said wearily. "The chemical was found in your husband's stomach. He swallowed it during the night, along with his medication. And you were alone with him. . . ."

He looked at her with a helpless expression. Who could deny the evidence? He had believed in Laura's innocence . . . but Hargest had convinced him that she was guilty. Finch felt disappointed and exhausted.

"But why would I have done something like that?" Laura asked, unable, once again, to understand the logic of these policemen.

"I'll tell you why," Hargest's cold voice replied. He launched into his explanation. "First of all, you cast your spell on Mr. Collins because he was a wealthy man. You were working in the glittering but hollow world of French fashion. You were stagnating and you decided to come to America to seek your fortune."

"That's not true! I came here to work—I was hired in Paris!"

"Keep quiet and listen if you want an answer to your question," Hargest spat. Laura was quiet and the detective continued. "Next, you invented some kind of crazy story about your so-called employment here. You probably wrote that contract yourself. During the trip over, you decided to try your luck with Mr. Collins. He was weak and ill and inclined to like you because you reminded him of his dead wife. You saw your opportunity and took advantage of it. But the ocean crossing didn't give you enough time to convince a reticent man, and by the time your ship reached New York, you still hadn't accomplished your project. Next, you extorted an invitation from Mr. Collins's nurse."

Laura was suddenly quiet at this interpretation of the facts; she remained calm, as if Hargest were talking to—and about—someone else.

"You managed to gain access to Silver Farm," he went on, "and you took advantage of Mr. Collins's weakness and the rest of the staff's naivety. In less than two months, you made yourself indispensable to the owner of the estate. Then you worked out the next part of your charade: you pretended you wanted to leave. A very clever move, Mrs. Collins. You know how to play the game. After much maneuvering, you led Mr. Collins to the altar and he made you his heiress. That's what you were after, and that's what you got."

Who are these people he's talking about, Laura wondered as Hargest's inevitable logic ran its course. *They're like characters in a detective novel. They can't be anyone I know.*

"Your idea was well executed," Hargest summed up. "But unfortunately for you, things didn't go according to plan. First, Mr. Collins was getting better. Every day, he seemed to grow stronger. You had the money, sure, but you were still chained to your husband, who was over twenty years older than you. He made you live at Silver Farm and the isolation of the place didn't sit well with you. You bought all kinds of pretty things at the start of your marriage, back when your husband opened a hefty bank account in your name, but what good is a beautiful dress if no one's there to admire it? No one but the people at Silver Farm, and you had no interest in them. You weren't after a back-door romance with a chauffeur. After all, you'd left your boyfriend back in France. So you decided to give fate a hand."

Hargest stopped, waiting for Laura's reaction. None came. She stared in disbelief, as if he had been telling her fairy tales and trying to pass them off as reality.

But despite her calm exterior, Laura's mind was working feverishly. She realized that everything she had said and done at Silver Farm—even the vague comments she'd made to Phyllis one lonely afternoon—had been distorted and turned against her. Everything was diabolically simple in Hargest's mind. He'd combed through her life, searching for details that might support his theory—and, of course, he'd found what he was looking for.

Keep calm, she told herself. *Don't let your rage boil over. That's what they're waiting for. They'll turn it into your confession.*

Hargest's implacable voice continued. "That's what you did, Mrs. Collins. Phyllis Baker handed your victim over to you. You couldn't have asked for a better opportunity. You're a woman of decision and you decided to take matters into your own hands. You had everything you needed for your little murder—an isolated house, with everyone away for the night. . . . Your victim was at your mercy, and your means was on a shelf in the garden shed. The only thing I don't understand is how you thought you could get away with it. How did you think you could ever hide it from us?"

Hargest was silent for a moment. Then, zeroing in on his victim, he said, "You gave your husband his medicine, but not with the usual glass of water—you poured two spoonfuls of poison into the water. It must have been easy. You just turned your back and dumped it in. He never once suspected his devoted spouse. And you'd crushed that whole bottle of tablets into the water, too. We've got the doctor's report: the overdose of medicine wouldn't have killed him so quickly. He might have been found the next morning, gasping for breath, and we could have saved him.

"But the weed killer is a lot more efficient; it worked immediately. Afterward, you left the empty bottle on the carpet near Mr. Collins's hand. The scene was set and you had no one to fear. You were alone in the house. You'd chased away the cook. But the whole thing was a little too neatly done. The doctor got suspicious and called in the police. . . . So much for the perfect crime, Mrs. Collins."

"No!" Laura spoke quietly, but her voice was powerful. "No," she said again. "It's not true!"

"Go get your things," Hargest ordered.

"Are you . . . arresting me?"

Finch put a gentle hand on her shoulder. "We're just taking you into custody . . . as a witness."

Hargest turned around. "What are you talking about?"

"You still have to prove this theory of yours," Finch said calmly. "You can't treat her like she's guilty. Innocent until proven guilty, remember?"

"She'll be a prisoner tomorrow once the district attorney interrogates her," Hargest spat. "My theory is flawless. This woman is a killer!"

The word "killer" rang in Laura's ears like a death knell. Suddenly she buried her face in her hands and sobbed.

"Do you want me to inform your family?" Finch asked kindly. "Someone who could help you out? I'm afraid you're in a tight spot."

She wiped the tears from her eyes. Her heart called out for Ross, silent and strong . . . but she fended off the impulse to seek him out.

Laura answered Finch's question in a level voice, head held high. "There is no one," she said, and walked proudly from the room.

Chapter 11

The long, lazy summer was coming to an end. Here and there, the lush green lawns of Paris were turning slowly to yellow and brown; a few trees showed an empty branch, the twigs looking naked and vulnerable. Brown and yellow leaves floated gently in the basins of the city's fountains.

A slow drizzle set in, soaking statues and awnings and forcing the cafés to retrieve their sidewalk tables. Pedestrians no longer strolled along the boulevards window-shopping. Umbrellas were opened, and people dashed from bistro to subway, heedless of the puddles.

Ross Montclair sat morosely in the window of a quiet café, watching the antics of his fellow Parisians as they tried to avoid getting wet. But he was paying little attention to the scene in front of him. He turned back to the table, took a sip of coffee and read again the teletype he had received shortly before his last broadcast. "Sidney Collins, American composer and conductor, found dead; suicide suspected." Ross read the enigmatic teletype over and over, trying to make sense of its message.

He hadn't heard a word from Laura since he'd received the wedding announcement two months ago. The announcement had shaken him badly and for a few days he had hoped it was a joke. Then, as time passed and no further word came, Ross was forced to realize that Laura really was married. With the realization came a sense of loneliness. He felt as though he had lost his only friend.

Ross had returned from Brussels in high spirits, looking forward eagerly to seeing Laura again. He had been miserable in the Belgian capital. The Common Market meetings had dragged on interminably and his hotel room had been drab, impersonal. He had spoken to no one for a week. On the plane home his mood had begun to lighten, and as he drove home from the airport his sense of anticipation had reached fever pitch. He would call Laura, ask her out for dinner. They would laugh about his horrible week, her boring job. . . . Ross parked and ran into his building, stopping at the mailbox on the way up to his apartment.

He tossed his mail onto the table and went to call Laura. There was no answer. Thinking he'd try again after a few moments, he sat down to read his mail.

The note from Laura stunned him. His girl friend was, at that moment, thousands of miles away . . . somewhere in the middle of the Atlantic Ocean. He couldn't believe she would make such a momentous decision without talking to him about it. Then he realized she *couldn't* talk to him—he hadn't been there. He had left town for selfish reasons—to think things over—and he had let her down.

For two months Ross's self-recriminations continued. The only person he felt comfortable with was Sonia,

Laura's roommate. Sonia listened as he talked about their relationship, analyzing his actions, Laura's actions, trying to make sense of Laura's departure. He fell into the habit of picking Sonia up after work—it was a comfortable routine, one he'd shared with Laura. Through all his talk Sonia was silent. *She understands*, Ross thought, *because she knows Laura, too.* They would see the occasional movie, share the occasional dinner. And Ross began to feel less lonely. He looked forward to Laura's return, never doubting she'd come back.

Then he received the wedding announcement, and his dream world came crashing down around him. For all their misunderstandings and arguments, in spite of their disagreements and bad timing, it never occurred to Ross that either of them would begin a separate life. He had believed, blindly, unquestioningly, that the day would come when both of them wanted the same thing at the same time, when his world and Laura's would be synchronized and become one.

Ross stirred his cold coffee and read the teletype again. It included the details of the discovery, stated the results of the autopsy and mentioned that the widow was being held for questioning. Ross sipped at his coffee, contemplating the piece of paper in front of him. Laura's husband was dead; Laura was in trouble. She was alone and friendless in a foreign country. True, she hadn't written to him in four months, and her silence had hurt his fragile pride. But his loyalty to her had never wavered.

Suddenly Ross gathered his papers and rushed out into the evening Paris drizzle. The thought of Laura locked in a cell, accused of poisoning her own husband, was more than he could bear. He returned to the staion in a frenzy.

"They're crazy over there!" he raged as he stormed through the station. He went directly to his boss and asked to be sent to cover the Collins affair, as the teletype had called it.

Ross Montclair had earned a reputation as a good, objective reporter, and his proposition was accepted. A ticket to New York would be waiting for him at the Paris airport.

On his way home to pack Ross stopped in to see Sonia, who insisted on accompanying him to the airport. She went back to his apartment with him. As he packed his bags Ross realized that Sonia was trying to dissuade him from his mission.

"Admit it," she said, "From what you've told me—and from what I've gathered—Laura married this guy for his money. All the motives are there—"

"Motives?" Ross was stunned. He couldn't believe that Sonia, Laura's friend—or so he had thought—would talk this way. "Those motives are pure fabrication!"

"How do you know?" Sonia asked coolly. "What if Laura's guilty? They don't arrest people for no reason. You'd look pretty ridiculous, running thousands of miles to defend a murderer!"

He turned on Sonia incredulously. "Guilty? Can you see Laura poisoning someone?"

"No more than I can see her marrying a decrepit old man because he's got millions of dollars," Sonia said spitefully.

Ross threw a handful of ties onto the suit jacket he'd folded and packed. He had no answer for Sonia; he was taken aback by her argument, and began to wonder what kind of person she was.

But Sonia demanded an answer. "Listen, Ross, you might as well face it—Laura's just not what you thought she was. Sometimes you misjudge people."

Ross looked her squarely in the eye. "You're right, Sonia. I *do* misjudge people."

Sonia began to smile, looking satisfied. But Ross hadn't finished talking yet.

"I'm glad you've been so honest with me this evening," he continued, "and your honesty has opened my eyes. The person I misjudged isn't Laura—it's you."

Sonia winced. "But you can't just take off for New York and leave me here. What about us?"

"Us? There's never been any 'us.' I trusted you, I talked to you because you were Laura's friend. But you're willing to forsake her—you'd let her rot in some foreign prison! Your part in this charade is over, Sonia—but thanks for your *concern*."

Ross picked up his suitcase and left the apartment.

WHEN HE ARRIVED IN New York, Ross began to gather information on the Collins affair with all the professional cool of a seasoned reporter. He'd traveled to the United States before and he knew exactly where to start. He talked with some colleagues in the news media, some old friends and the officials at the French Consulate. He learned that Laura was still being held in the West Cornwall jail, and he also learned that a state lawyer had been appointed to defend her.

The lawyer's name was Edward Higgins, a young man who shared an office with several other aspiring attorneys. Ross liked him immediately. Higgins was a rugged, hearty fellow who would look more at home on a football field than in a lawyer's chambers. He had curly red hair and warm blue eyes, and he extended a welcoming hand when Ross came into the room. But when the reporter told him why he was there, the lawyer's smile faded.

"It's a difficult case, Mr. Montclair."

"You've looked over all the documents?"

"Yes, and everything in my file has been reported in the papers."

"Then I can't believe they arrested Lau—Mrs. Collins," Ross said firmly. "I read all those accounts, and I've examined all the notices and communiqués that didn't make it into the papers. I haven't found anything that proves the murder charge against Lau—I mean, Mrs. Collins. She was in the house, she gave her husband his medicine, but that's all. No one actually saw her touch the poison. If Mr. Collins had wanted to kill himself, he could have done it. Nothing proves it wasn't suicide."

"You're forgetting the circumstantial evidence. She was alone with her husband on the night he died. She ordered the poison that killed him. And she stands to inherit millions from his death. That's enough to make anyone think twice."

Ross shook his head sadly.

"Find the motive and you've found the criminal," Higgins said. "That's what all the detectives in the murder mysteries say . . . and I'm afraid it's probably true in this case."

"But all this is only theory," Ross protested. "The evidence is purely circumstantial. I suppose the judge has set bail."

"He did set it, after the preliminary hearing . . . but another event has influenced things. It hasn't hit the papers yet, but it will tonight."

"What event? What's happened?"

"Collins's brother, Robert Collins, is suing for civil injury—on top of the criminal charges."

"Collins had a brother? I hadn't heard that."

"No one's ever mentioned him until now. Evidently the two brothers hadn't seen each other for years. Robert was quite a hell-raiser and he managed to get himself disinherited. He's been bumming around doing all kinds of things—keeper of a gambling house, mercenary, taxi driver—you know the type. He even spent a little time in jail. At last count, he was a tour guide organizer. He showed up two days ago and announced he was going to launch a civil suit against Mrs. Collins. He seems bound and determined to have her found guilty of criminal negligence . . . or murder."

"It's a little late to start defending his brother now, isn't it? I suppose he stands to gain something."

Higgins smiled. "Of course. What did you expect? If the widow is found guilty, she loses her right to inherit the deceased's estate. Everything goes to the next of kin—unless the will names a second benefactor."

"So there's at least one other person besides Mrs. Collins who'd benefit from Sidney's death, right?"

Higgins shook his head. Theoretically, yes. But I'm afraid it's not that simple. Robert was thousands of miles away when his brother died—he spent the night playing blackjack in Monte Carlo. He couldn't be in two places at once, you know."

For the first time since he'd arrived in New York, Ross began to feel discouraged. His sense of hopelessness increased as he listened to the lawyer: it was obvious that

Higgins was inclined to consider his own client guilty. The evidence, even though circumstantial, seemed insurmountable.

Ross was devastated. His belief in Laura's innocence was so strong that he couldn't understand how anyone would think she was guilty. But Ross seemed to be a minority of one—even Higgins remained unconvinced.

"I think the most sensible option is for Mrs. Collins to plead guilty," Higgins said. "We can make a case for temporary insanity, and she would be examined by psychiatrists. Our only other option would be to call it a crime of passion—and we obviously can't do that. The witnesses all agree that there wasn't much warmth in their marriage. They slept in separate rooms and never appeared in public as man and wife." Higgins shrugged resignedly. "They made a pretty strange couple. I'm afraid that, when the prosecutor points all this out to the jury, things are going to look pretty bad for my client. The jury will believe what everyone's saying, that Mrs. Collins married for money."

By the time Ross left the lawyer's office he was totally demoralized. But he was an optimist by nature, and he refused to give up completely. He went back to his hotel room and began to make some phone calls. In a short time, he had managed to get permission to visit Laura at the jail the next morning. He didn't sleep that night. One scheme after another tantalized him, and he was haunted by the gray shadow of the prison walls. By the time he closed his eyes, his travel alarm clock was ringing.

ROSS SAT NERVOUSLY in the austere visiting chambers of the jail. He looked up from his newspaper and saw two figures approaching him. One was a hefty female guard.

At first Ross didn't recognize the second woman. She was walking toward him with a dull tread, her emaciated face hollow and lifeless. Then he realized it was Laura.

"You have fifteen minutes," the guard announced, abandoning her prisoner in front of Ross and taking up her position by the door.

They stood staring at one another. For a moment, neither Ross nor Laura spoke. Her clothes were wrinkled and stained, her hair was matted, her skin was dead white. There were deep circles under her eyes. The two friends were silent, both hesitant to speak to each other in this nightmare setting.

Finally Ross broke this silence. "Laura, what's going on? Is it really you? What happened?"

She nodded her head wearily. "Yes, Ross, it's me."

She was stiff and expressionless, but to Ross she seemed as tightly wound as a watch spring. Yet she looked exhausted, and her face was etched with fatigue. She maintained a delicate balance for a few seconds. Then her tenuous poise deserted her.

"Oh, Ross, Ross!"

She stumbled to him and he caught her in his arms. He pressed her thin, fragile body to his chest as her tears flowed. "Laura, don't cry," he whispered into her ear. "Laura, darling."

He felt her body shiver and stiffen. "I'm not your darling anymore . . . I'm a common criminal—they think I'm a murderer!"

Sobs racked her frail form as she clung to Ross. Then she pulled away from him and wiped the tears from her eyes. "But you . . . do you believe it, too?"

Suddenly Ross laughed. His laughter echoed in the

somber room, and seemed to chase a few of the shadows away. In her corner, the guard raised an eyebrow.

"You've got to be kidding, Laura. How could I ever believe a thing like that? I haven't lost my mind since you left me. I've been mad, angry, even furious—but not mindless!"

Ross's laughter seemed to clear the air. "I did leave you," she repeated, as if she were realizing it for the first time. "Why did I do that?"

"I don't know, my flighty friend. Just one of your whims, I suppose."

With his finger, he tried to smooth away a worry line at the corner of her mouth. Then he kissed away one last teardrop. "One day we started in at each other over the phone. Why? I don't even remember. Some kind of stupid quarrel. We were both keyed up and we had words—"

"But we did that a hundred times and we never broke up. I don't understand what happened. . . ."

"Both of us were pushing too hard," Ross told her. "The resistance came from my side, too. I went off to Brussels without talking to you. That's where all the trouble started. And then when I came back—the lady had vanished. The next time I see you, you're married, widowed and a prisoner. In four months you've gone through quite a number of transformations. I always knew you were special, but I don't know how you managed this one!"

"Five minutes left," the guard said monotonously, bringing them back to reality.

Laura grabbed Ross's arm and lowered her voice to a desperate whisper. "Ross, you're not going to leave me here, are you? It's . . . it's horrible!"

Fighting against his own despair and the desolation he knew Laura was feeling, Ross tried to comfort her. "Of course I'll get you out of here. This is no place for a vacation. I'll do everything in my power . . . and I promise you it won't take long."

"I didn't kill him, Ross," Laura pleaded. "You . . . you do believe me, don't you?"

"I know, Laura, I believe you, darling. Now here's what I want you to do. In the first place, remember I love you. Right? Forget the past four months. And Laura, you have to be strong. I know this place is no picnic, but you'll have to put up with it for a little while longer. Laura, you trust me, don't you? Because I've come here for you, to help you. . . ."

"Okay, Ross, I'll be strong . . . at least, I'll try. And I trust you. But they will let me out of here, won't they?"

"Of course they will, sweetheart." Ross answered with more conviction than he felt. He held her close and kissed her hollow cheeks and trembling mouth. He felt an overwhelming desire to comfort her, to give her enough strength to help her through this nightmare. "Don't worry, darling. Pretty soon we'll be on the plane back to France."

"Time's up," the guard's voice rang out. "Please come this way, Mrs. Collins."

Mrs. Collins. . . . Ross watched as Laura was led away. Mrs. Collins. Ross hated that name. As he walked out of the prison he looked around him. People hurried by, pigeons fluttered from telephone wire to sidewalk, sparrows twittered in the hedges. Suddenly Ross was more determined than ever to help Laura. He wouldn't give up till she was free.

Chapter 12

Ross had his work cut out for him, and he soon realized that it wasn't going to be easy. His first problem was time. Laura's hearing was scheduled for Friday. For four days she would be held without bail, without any contact with the outside world. In four days Ross hoped to do what Laura's lawyer and the police had been unable to do: prove her innocence.

His second problem was his job. He wanted to convince the world that Laura was innocent, and he would gladly have written a thousand articles to accomplish just that. But he was being paid to report the facts—and the facts looked increasingly grim. For two days Ross did his homework. He tracked down as many of the people involved as he could, kept in touch with Laura's lawyer and read everything that appeared in the papers.

The murder was front-page news. The summer had been quiet—a few fires, the usual bank robberies—there hadn't been anything spectacular for four long, hot months. So the story of Silver Farm had caught the public's imagination. People were following the case in the papers. Some of them were betting four to one that

Laura was guilty. Others disagreed with the odds, but she was undoubtedly everyone's number-one suspect. One journalist used the phrase "the poisonous spouse" several times in his article, and several reporters had begun to refer to Mrs. Collins as "the Herbex murderer."

Ross found the cynicism of his American colleagues discouraging at first. Soon, however, his discouragement turned to resentment, then anger. The other French journalists, aware of his personal involvement in the case, did their best to calm him down. They knew that a show of temper would do his reputation no good.

One of these journalists was Roger Parent, an old friend of Ross's from Paris. He, like Ross, believed in Laura's innocence implicitly.

"We'll get her out of this," Roger said. "The accusation is trumped up—anyone can see that. It wouldn't stand up to serious questioning—there's no positive proof."

Ross agreed fervently. But how could a pair of French journalists fight the ever-increasing tide of public opinion? People seemed to be eager for blood and scandal. To make matters worse, there were a few unscrupulous journalists who seemed determined to comply with public opinion. They did an interview with Phyllis Baker and many papers, even the most responsible, ran it on page one. The photo that accompanied the story added to Phyllis Baker's credibility. In her white cap she had an air of respectability, and she looked like the perfect nurse.

The article itself was nothing more than an inflated accusation of Collins's wife, told from the nurse's point of view. To increase the reader's sympathy, Miss Baker took herself to task, lamenting her role in the affair. The article made one thing plain: Phyllis Baker was an altruistic woman motivated only by her sense of right and justice. In her attempts to convince her readers of this, she asked them to consider her own circumstances. "I hope you can see," the article concluded, "that I have nothing to gain for myself. I wish only to see that justice is done, so that this country will be safe—for you and your children."

This article appeared under banner headlines on Wednesday morning. All that day Ross barely managed to control his temper. By suppertime he was waiting impatiently for the evening editions to appear. When they did he finally lost the last bit of restraint he had. Robert Collins had decided to jump on the publicity bandwagon.

Ross didn't need to open a paper to read the latest article; it appeared directly under the name of several of the major newspapers. WHEELS OF JUSTICE NEED OILING, the syndicated headline stated. The slow progress of the preliminary hearings had exasperated Robert Collins. But the victim's brother obviously felt comfortable in the limelight. He had fielded the reporters' questions dexterously, managing to use the word "murder" seven times in four paragraphs. Like Phyllis Baker, he was "concerned only with finding out the truth." He was determined "to pursue his brother's murderer to the bitter end—till justice is done."

For Ross Montclair, a new stage of the fight had begun. Until that Wednesday evening, he had been content to villify the press only in the company of his compatriots. But Robert Collins's statements enraged him, and he accepted them as a declaration of war. He went to Roger's place to discuss the situation and plan a method of attack.

They didn't have much to go on. Finally, discouraged and embittered, Ross decided to go home. He and Roger hadn't come up with any definite plans, but they had a better idea of what they wanted to accomplish. Someone—they didn't know who, and it would have to be someone who was not involved in the case—someone should speak up for Laura. Already, in the public's eyes, she was "the defendant." Perhaps some anonymous judge could be interviewed and quoted as saying that, in truth, no one had been accused of anything yet, and the spate of damning articles was prejudiced and unethical.

Roger walked his friend to the door, advising patience and telling Ross not to get discouraged. Ross laughed bitterly.

"Well, it's obvious I'm not going to get anything done tonight—I can't even think straight, I'm so tired. What we really need is some new evidence. Maybe some fingerprints on the lock on the shed door—or some local who saw something through his binoculars but didn't want to say anything, so he wouldn't get involved. . . ." There was a long pause as Ross looked at Roger sheepishly. "Yeah, I know—too farfetched, right?"

Roger laughed. "Well, my friend, until tonight I never thought you were the type who went in for miracles."

"That's all we need, isn't it?" Ross asked sadly. "The woman I love is in jail and I can't help her—it would take a bloody miracle to get her out." He smiled wryly. "Well, I don't know about you, but I'm going to go home and start praying."

The phone began to ring as Ross was unlocking the door of his hotel room. He knew it had to be important for someone to call this late at night. In his excitement, he dropped his keys and the pile of newspapers he was carrying landed on top of them. He retrieved the keys, fumbled the lock open and ran across the room to the phone. He snatched the receiver up just in time to hear the click and buzz of the dial tone as his caller hung up. "Damn!" Ross muttered, and threw the phone across the room in disgust. His attempts to make himself believe that it had been a wrong number were unsuccessful. As he fell asleep, he became increasingly convinced that that phone call would have turned the case around.

ROSS WOKE UP Thursday morning with that phone call nagging at the back of his mind. As he shaved and dressed in his other suit, he thought ruefully of the closet full of clothes back in his apartment—thousands of miles away. *If I don't go to the dry cleaner's soon*, he thought, *I'll be out of a job—no one will let me get close enough for an interview.*

He ran down the stairs to the hotel coffee shop and grabbed a quick breakfast while he went over his schedule for the day. He had managed to get an interview with Inspector Finch, the detective who had first investigated the case, and he had to be in Connecticut by lunchtime.

He bought a few newspapers on his way to the bus station, got his ticket and found the right bus, then settled back to read the latest developments in the life of the woman he loved. . . .

Six hours later, a very discouraged Ross Montclair climbed off the bus in New York City. His interview with Inspector Finch had been disappointing. The detective readily admitted that initially he thought Laura was innocent. Even after he'd interviewed the nurse and chauffeur, he'd hoped that Mrs. Collins would be able to prove her innocence. But the circumstantial evidence had been too overwhelming—and besides, Mrs. Collins was the only one with any kind of motive. The more he had thought about it, the inspector told Ross, the more a million-dollar inheritance seemed like a valid motive. So he'd handed the case over to his superiors, and Ross knew the rest.

Ross had thanked him and left, realizing as he got on the bus that he'd forgotten to take his suit to the dry cleaner's. And that phone call was still tantalizing his imagination. And he didn't have even the beginnings of a story to file. . . . *To hell with this business*, he thought disgustedly as he walked through the four-o'clock crush downtown. The discouraged journalist turned in at the next bar, determined to forget his problems by drowning them in a gallon or two of American beer.

He succeeded. By the time he got back to his hotel it was midnight. Outside his room, he tried to decide which of the three keyholes he should stick his key into; once he'd solved that problem he had to select one of the three doorknobs. As he was reaching for the third doorknob the phone started to ring. Two minutes later it stopped just as Ross, still on the wrong side of the door, was triumphantly turning the knob.

For the second time in two days, Ross fell asleep thinking about a phone call.

ON FRIDAY MORNING, at ten o'clock, Laura Collins was indicted on a charge of first-degree murder.

Chapter 13

The old building stood majestically in the middle of seven acres of Connecticut woodland. It was made of stone, a worn, darkish gray in color, and surrounded by hedges and ancient trees. In the fading light of the late-September sun the trees were brilliantly colored, yellow, orange and scarlet. They cast long shadows on the building, making it appear slightly forbidding. The last few dying rays of the sun reached the west wall of the building and touched one of the windows, turning it bloodred.

Laura Collins stood at the window, her face framed by two vertical iron bars. The cold iron touched her cheekbones. There were four bars in the small window. Her fingers curled around the outer two, her thumbs white from the tightness of her grip.

She stood on a wooden bench. It had two deep depressions in its center, directly under the window, worn by the feet of countless people who had climbed onto the bench to stare out past the cold stone walls into the woodland.

In front of the bench was an old wooden table, its surface scarred and worn. A few feet from the table was an iron cot, its thin mattress covered with a torn blanket. In the corner across from the window, fastened to the east wall, was a small sink with a cup, a toothbrush and a bar of soap. There was no other furniture in the room.

Four feet of wall separated the sink from the cell door. The door was made of bars, eight vertical and six horizontal, and had no knob or handle. As Laura stood looking out the window, a key was inserted in the lock of her door and a guard entered, carrying a tray. Laura turned and watched as the guard set the tray on the table. The guard turned and left the room, pulling the door shut with a metallic clang. Laura turned back to the window.

The sun finally sank below the horizon; Laura did not move. The guard returned, checked that none of the utensils was missing, and removed the tray of uneaten food. The trees were only vaguely illuminated by the moon when Laura climbed from the bench and walked the four steps to her bed.

ON TUESDAY MORNING Ross dropped his suit off at the cleaner's. Then he went to see Mr. Higgins again. Laura's lawyer was pessimistic, but firm. He had no new facts, no new ideas, no new angles. He had done everything he could think of, he told the young reporter.

"Everything short of helping Laura," Ross answered cynically.

Mr. Higgins kept his temper. "The primary problem," he said, "is motive. How can I help Mrs. Collins when everything points to her? No one else had anything to gain by Mr. Collins's death, so naturally. . . ."

Before he could begin speaking again, Ross asked him

bluntly, "Have you gone over the will? What happens if Laura's found guilty? Does she still inherit?"

The lawyer smiled wryly. "Unfortunately, no. The court would read the will as though Mrs. Collins were . . . dead."

"And?" Ross persisted in his question. "And if Laura *was* . . . dead, who would inherit? It seems to me that if everyone thinks Laura could have killed this guy for a million bucks, someone else could have done the same thing."

"It's a good idea, Ross, but there's a slight problem with it."

"What?"

"The person who stands to inherit, in the event that my client is . . . unavailable, is the deceased's brother. I went over the will after our last conversation on this topic. We've already discussed the problems—and Robert still has an alibi."

Ross looked at the lawyer, feeling slightly foolish. He had come on like the heavy in a Perry Mason rerun, not giving Mr. Higgins any credit for having done his job, spouting theories like some television detective. And the lawyer had already thought things out. "Mr. Higgins, I'm sorry," Ross said. "I guess this whole thing is beginning to get to me."

"I can understand that, Ross, and I don't blame you for snapping at me. It must seem to you like we're working at cross-purposes. You're trying to get Mrs. Collins out of jail, and I'm acting on the assumption that she's going to stay there. I don't mean to discourage you, but all I'm concerned with right now is trying to get my client the most reasonable sentence possible under the circumstances."

Ross gaped at the lawyer. "But they can't prove

anything! Laura didn't do it! I *know* Laura—I *know* she didn't do anything!"

"Calm down, Ross, calm down. The district attorney's office has a very solid circumstantial case—"

"Circumstantial! What about proof? What about witnesses? What about evidence? What about your great legal system we keep hearing about? What about innocent until *proven* guilty? Nobody can prove anything!"

"Ross, your Gallic temper is not helping the situation," the lawyer snapped. After a moment he continued more patiently. "Now listen, Ross, everything you've said is right—we both know that. But I want you to put yourself in the shoes of the jury for a minute. The one reason you're so sure of your argument is—as you said yourself—that you *know* Laura. So pretend, for a minute, that you don't. Look at the facts—and remember, there's a million dollars at stake."

"So that's the way American justice works," Ross said bitterly.

"No, Ross," the lawyer answered, "that's the way the world works."

SEVERAL HOURS LATER, Ross repeated the conversation to Roger as they watched the six-o'clock news at Roger's apartment. Ross was vehemently proposing a new scheme: he wanted to hire a French lawyer to come and defend Laura.

"Ross, forget it!" Roger answered. "One of our lawyers in a Hartford court? Are you serious? They wouldn't let him open his mouth!"

"Okay, Roger, you're right, as usual. But what are we going to do?"

"Well, we'll just have to come up with something else, I guess."

"Like what?"

"Like . . . like some new piece of evidence or something. Something that will prove Laura's innocence—something that will make the truth show through."

"Don't count on it," Ross answered as he prepared to leave. "We're in bad shape, Roger. And I'm beginning to think there's nothing I can do."

Ross walked out the door and down the stairs. When he reached the sidewalk he started walking uncertainly in the direction of his hotel. The evening was warm. As he walked along, he took his jacket off and slung it over his shoulder.

He looked around him. The sun was setting, touching the skyscrapers and streets with a hazy orange glow. Something was teasing his mind. He stood still in the middle of the sidewalk, lost in thought. He couldn't figure out what was bothering him . . . it was like something he'd forgotten to do, something he'd forgotten to think about. *I took my suit to the cleaner's,* he thought, *so that's not it.*

He started to walk again, still thinking. *I filed yesterday's story, I spoke to the lawyer, I watched the news, I ate. . . . That's it. Dinner. I forgot to eat dinner.* He stopped and looked around. He wasn't too sure where he was—he hadn't been paying attention to the direction his feet were taking him. Across the street he saw a diner. It looked reasonably inviting, so he crossed the street, went in, sat down at the counter and studied the menu.

A half hour later, after asking directions from the

man behind the cash register, Ross left the diner. He strolled along the New York streets, somewhat pleased with his ability to cope with the metropolis. The evening had grown cool. As Ross put his jacket back on, he was again struck by the feeling that there was something he'd forgotten to do. His footsteps quickened. The dinner had appeased his appetite, but there was still something else bothering him. "Damn!" Ross said under his breath. "This is going to drive me crazy!" He smiled politely at an elderly woman, who had heard him muttering and was openly staring at him. *Maybe it already has*, he thought wryly.

By the time he was within a few blocks of his hotel, Ross realized that he didn't want to go up to his room. He stopped, looking around uncertainly, wondering where to go. He didn't feel like drinking, that was for sure. Last time he'd gotten drunk. . . . Ross couldn't quite put his finger on what had gone wrong last time he'd gotten drunk, but he knew it wouldn't help. He finally decided to see a movie. It would distract him, make him stop thinking for a few hours. He retraced his steps and went into the nearest theater.

Ross COULD HEAR his phone ringing as he got off the elevator on his floor of the hotel. He started to run for his room, reaching into his pocket for his keys as he ran. Before he could even get the key in the lock, the ringing had stopped.

ON WEDNESDAY MORNING, as Ross was on his way out of the hotel, the desk clerk called his name and beckoned him over. Curious, Ross walked toward the desk. The clerk had gotten off his stool and was busily digging through a pile of envelopes, newspapers and magazines.

"Just a moment, Mr. Montclair. I know it's right here somewhere . . . special delivery envelope came in for you this morning," he explained to the puzzled journalist. "Ah, here it is. I signed for it myself, so you're all set to go."

"Thanks a lot," Ross told the clerk, then headed toward the dining room for coffee. He glanced curiously at the envelope. It was large, about a foot square, thick and seemed to be reinforced with cardboard. It had more Fragile and Do Not Bend stickers on it that Ross had ever seen outside a post office. There was enough postage on it to send it around the world twice—and the postage stamps were French. On the back of the envelope, half-buried under two exhortations to treat the package carefully, Ross found the return address. Paris. He didn't recognize the street address.

His coffee came, and after taking a sip, Ross carefully opened the envelope. Gently he slid out two pieces of ordinary shirt cardboard, which looked as if they had an entire roll of masking tape wrapped around them, and several sheets of plain, unlined white paper. Ross took another sip of his coffee, realized he'd forgotten to add cream, poured liberally from the pitcher on the table, took another sip and burned his tongue. Half-afraid of being disappointed by their content, he tentatively touched the sheets of paper then picked them up and began to read.

Dear Mr. Montclair,

This is the first time I've ever sent a letter to America. It feels kind of strange, sending a letter right across the ocean. What's it like in New York

City? My magazines say that's where all the movie stars live—except the ones in California, of course.

Ross stopped reading and toyed idly with his coffee spoon. He thought for a moment, then turned to the last page of the letter, looking for a signature. It was scrawled in three-inch letters across the bottom half of the page: Zizi. *What on earth could Zizi be sending me,* he wondered. His hopes fading, he was about to abandon the letter when his eye caught the words "Nice" and "Baker" as he shuffled the pages. Intrigued, Ross turned again to the first page.

But of course, I'm not writing to you about movie stars—unless you count Delia Marston as a star. Only I'm not writing about Delia Marston, either— I mean, not really. What I'm really writing about is that time Laura and I went to Nice, for the Monestier wedding, if you recall. I guess Laura didn't get a chance to tell you about the man on the train—a real creep, if you ask me. He's the one who kept asking me if Laura was Delia Marston, the movie star, only he wouldn't believe me when I said no.

Ross wondered vaguely what Zizi was talking about. He reached for his coffee, blew on it to cool it and took a large gulp. It was almost cold. He beckoned to the waiter and ordered more, thinking about Zizi's letter. What was it Laura used to call her? Zizi of the magic fingers, that was it. *Well, she may have magic fingers, and even a magic tongue,* Ross thought, *but she'll never make it as a journalist.* The waiter brought his coffee.

Ross barely looked at it as he went back to his reading.

Anyway, Mr. Montclair, you probably don't know what I'm talking about so I'll try to tell you. This creep that kept hanging around Laura—well, I saw him again, after the wedding, while I was seeing the sights of Nice. You remember I had my camera with me? I took pictures of everything—the town, the church and stuff. And I took a picture of this creep. He was with some woman, right? So just for the fun of it, I took his picture, and that's why I'm writing to you.

Totally bewildered, Ross set the letter on the table. *Thanks a lot, Zizi,* he thought. *At least now I know there are two women in the world who can drive me to distraction from four thousand miles away.* Determined to enjoy his coffee before Zizi distracted him again, Ross reached for his cup. He sipped gratefully, then picked the letter up once more.

I know what you're thinking—what is this girl talking about, right? Well, Mr. Montclair, take a look at this picture I took. I got her face enlarged, just so you'd see what I mean. Remember I said the creep was with someone? A woman? Well, it wasn't just *any* woman — it was that nurse in the newspaper. The hard-looking one who said all those things about Laura. Mind you, in my picture she's not all dried-up looking and serious like she is in the newspaper. But it's her, all right.

So that's what I wanted to tell you. If the police want to know, the wedding was on April third—I mean, so you know when I took the picture. I read that nurse article in the paper and couldn't believe the things she said about Laura—it's just not true, she wouldn't do something like that. So I'm hoping this picture will help her out.

I'm going to telephone you to tell you this package is on the way, so you can get to work right away, digging up information and interviewing people like you do on TV. I hope you can help Laura, we're all worried about her, and if you see any movie stars, maybe you can take some pictures for me.

Anyway, I'll talk to you on the phone pretty soon, in case you want to ask me some questions.

Yours, Zizi

Ross toyed with his empty coffee cup. He was excited by Zizi's information and eager to show the photographs to Laura's lawyer. The only problem was that, as far as Ross could tell, the young woman's information was totally useless. He knew, from reading the files on the whole case, that Miss Baker had claimed she was with Sidney Collins from January until August. And that in April, the nurse had stated she was at her patient's bedside in Switzerland. But so what? *Even a nurse is entitled to a few days off now and then*, Ross told himself sternly. *Don't go getting all excited over nothing—think about this thing logically.*

He looked up, caught the waiter's eye and motioned for more coffee. Then, very carefully, with the handle of his spoon, Ross slit open the cardboard sheets Zizi had sent him. He set the top layer of cardboard on the table and turned over the first sheet in the packet. It was the picture of Phyllis Baker that had appeared in the papers. He propped it carefully against the sugar bowl, then returned to the packet. He turned over a snapshot. It was of two people, a man and a woman. The man was smiling and the woman, who clung tightly to the man's arm, was laughing. Ross propped the snapshot against the salt shaker and almost gingerly lifted the last item from the cardboard. It was a face—a woman's face. There was nothing else in the picture—no background, no man—just the face. Ross stared, then reached for the newspaper clipping.

Zizi was right, there was no doubt about it. Ross carefully compared her enlargement to the grainy newspaper photograph. It was as if there were two Miss Bakers. The expressions on her face in the two pictures were as different as night and day, and her hair was different, too, but the photographs were of the same woman. Ross was amazed at Zizi's acuity—it took an experienced eye to see the similarity of features in the two faces. In the newspaper, the woman's hair was pulled back tightly under a nurse's cap and the face was severe. In Zizi's picture the woman's eyes were made up, her mouth was open in generous laughter and her hair formed a blond cloud around her face. But despite the superficial differences, the features were the same.

So there are two Miss Bakers, Ross thought. *But where does that really get me? Just because she has a private life, lets herself enjoy life once in a while—there's nothing wrong with that.*

Slightly discouraged, Ross examined the three photographs again, then slid them back in the brown envelope. He folded Zizi's letter and tucked it away in his pocket, then sat back to drink his third cup of coffee.

He decided to take Zizi's information to Roger, to see what his friend thought, before he went to the lawyer. If Roger thought they had something, he would contact Higgins. In the meantime, he didn't want to embarrass himself in front of the lawyer again—once had been enough.

Ross finished his coffee, paid the bill and walked quickly to Roger's place. He took the stairs two at a time, knocked peremptorily and walked into the apartment before Roger had a chance to open the door. He accepted his fourth cup of coffee that morning from his friend who was, as usual, writing his story in front of the television. There was a talk show on, he told Ross, and one of the guests was Robert Collins. Ross sat down with his back to the set and began telling Roger about Zizi's letter. He'd given Roger Zizi's enlarged photograph and the newspaper clipping, and was holding the snapshot delicately in his left hand. Roger was comparing the two pictures when he glanced up at the TV.

"Here he is, Ross—Robert Collins, the famous brother."

Ross turned slightly in his chair and froze as he saw the television screen. He was staring into the eyes of the man in Zizi's snapshot.

Chapter 14

Every morning at twenty after ten the inmates of the Midstone Women's Penitentiary began to move out into the exercise yard, a square of ground directly behind the old stone building. The women exercised in groups. Each row of cells in the prison was called a tier, and the women were sent outside tier by tier. There were seven tiers at Midstone, and each contained eight cells. Each tier remained outside for twenty minutes: from twenty-past ten until twenty-past twelve, there were sixteen prisoners walking, jogging or shuffling around the small square of hard-packed earth.

For these two hours the guards were alert to the slightest sign of trouble. Quiet conversation was allowed, but any demonstration of exuberance was frowned upon.

By twelve-twenty the guards relaxed. The seventh tier—the ground level of the west wing—contained only one inmate. She was not like the other inmates; she was not a prisoner in the conventional sense. Although Midstone was a minimum-security institution, it still functioned as all prisons do: it protected the outside world from any damage its inmates might do. The woman in tier seven was in Midstone because the state of Connecticut had wanted to protect her from the outside world.

Since her arrival at Midstone she had had to be led out to the yard by a guard. Every day for twenty-three days she had stepped timidly through the door to the yard, looked around confusedly and walked to the wooden bench in the shelter of the south wall. She would sit there quietly, hands folded, waiting patiently for her guard to lead her back to her cell.

As soon as the cell door was shut behind tier seven the guards went to the cafeteria to watch the inmates during lunch. The women sat on benches at long, linoleum-covered tables, again tier by tier, six tiers in all. Each day one guard was assigned the task of carrying a tray to tier seven. Tier seven was totally isolated from the other inmates.

And with good reason. Twenty-three days ago, the woman in tier seven had been led into the Midstone Women's Penitentiary by several Hartford policemen. She had arrived shortly after one o'clock, and the police had taken her through the cafeteria on their way to the west wing. As the woman had walked hesitantly between the uniformed men, the prisoners at the tables had grown ominously quiet. Then tier five had begun to jeer and shout, and other tiers had picked up the chant: "Weed killer! Weed killer!" One enterprising young woman from tier three had picked up her egg salad sandwich and flung it in the direction of the newcomer. The missile found its mark.

As the guards did their best to quell the uproar, the policemen led their sobbing charge to the west wing.

Since that day, tier seven had been isolated from the rest of the prison.

Since that day, the woman in tier seven had not spoken.

LAURA COLLINS was standing on the wooden bench, hands tightly gripping the iron bars in the window, when the guard entered her cell and set her lunch tray on the table. Laura didn't move. She waited tensely for the metallic clang of the cell door as it closed behind the guard. Several seconds went by as Laura nervously clung to the cold iron bars. Finally, curious, she turned.

The guard was standing beside the table, her fingers delicately tracing the imprints in the scarred wood. She glanced quickly at the woman on the bench, then stepped back and leaned against the cell wall, her shoulders flat against the stone. She reached into the breast pocket of her tunic and took out a pack of cigarettes and a lighter. Placing a cigarette between her lips, she lighted it carefully, eyeing her prisoner guardedly. Before Laura could turn back to the window the guard stepped forward and extended the cigarettes and the lighter.

"Do you smoke?" she asked politely.

"Th-thank you," Laura replied, surprised by the guard's informality. She accepted the cigarette and a light, then blushed as she realized she had broken her vow of silence. She climbed down off her bench and sat at the table, inhaling the cigarette luxuriously.

After a few moments she looked up at the guard timidly, expecting to see avid curiosity on the older woman's face. But the guard was smoking peacefully, staring out the window. She finished her cigarette, put it out and reached into her pocket again. She set two cigarettes on the table at Laura's elbow, beside the lunch tray.

"I'll be back in half an hour. If the food on that tray hasn't been eaten, I'll expect an explanation." She placed a book of matches on the table beside the cigarettes, turned and left the room.

The cell door clanged hollowly behind her.

For the first time in twenty-three days, the woman in tier seven ate her lunch.

Laura had been living in a world of silence for three weeks. She remembered, as she lighted one of the cigarettes the guard had left her, when the silence had begun—and she remembered the nightmarish chaos that had preceded the silence of the prison.

Thirty days ago, Laura had been taken to the state courthouse in Hartford. It was a vast new building, made of granite, glass and chrome. As she climbed the steps between two policemen Laura had looked back over her shoulder at the busy downtown street, the rush of traffic, the fountains with their pools filled with fallen leaves. The policemen had been patient, gently touching her elbows to guide her into the building and down the long, polished tile hallway.

They had taken an elevator to the third floor, turned left and led her into a large, busy room lighted by fluorescent bulbs. There were about thirty people in the room: several judges, eight or ten lawyers, three clerks, the district attorney, some men in business suits. . . . Finally Laura caught sight of Mr. Higgins, her own lawyer, and his assistant. Inspector Finch was there, too, and that impatient partner of his. Laura didn't recognize anyone else.

After about half an hour Laura began to wonder if she

was in the right room after all. No one had spoken to her, and no one seemed to be interested in her. She had expected her preliminary hearing to be brief, dry and totally formal. This crowded, noisy room upset her.

She turned to the policeman on her right to ask him if he knew what was going on. But before she finished her question the hubbub in the room died down, and everyone looked expectantly at the district attorney.

He was a thin, patient-looking man, with gray hair and arched eyebrows. His voice surprised Laura. She had expected a dusty but businesslike voice after seeing his face. But when he spoke it was in rich, mellifluous tones. His voice was beautiful. *I wish he were my lawyer*, Laura thought, *and that we had a jury full of young, impressionable women—I'd believe anything that voice told me.*

The voice was telling her, and everyone else in the room, that the state believed she, Laura Collins, had rationally and cold-bloodedly killed her husband. Laura listened, shocked, as the even, cultured voice repeated the circumstantial evidence indicating her guilt. She tried to stand, to deny the things the district attorney was saying, but the policemen held her elbows. She couldn't move.

Mr. Higgins, noticing her distress, moved to her side and bent to reassure her. She looked at him blindly, unable to concentrate on his words. The voice of the district attorney still held its audience captive.

That can't be me he's describing, Laura thought, beginning to panic. *He's never even spoken to me.* She stared at the man's face. As if feeling her eyes on him, he turned and met her stare. Mr. Higgins quickly stepped between his client and the district attorney.

After what seemed an eternity to Laura, the man stopped speaking. She heard someone say, "Mr. Higgins?" and her lawyer went up and talked quietly to the judge for a few moments. Laura sat still, expecting her lawyer to deny the district attorney's arguments. He would speak logically, truthfully, and he would make the people in the room stop staring at her as if she were some kind of criminal.

But Mr. Higgins didn't make a speech. He turned and caught her eye, shaking his head. The judge banged on his desk with a little hammer and said something Laura didn't understand. Her two attendants touched her arms, and Laura was led out into the hall. The room began to empty, and finally Mr. Higgins came out, in the middle of an animated conversation with his assistant, the district attorney and the judge.

The four men approached her and Laura, suddenly frightened, took a step backward. Her two policemen once again took her arms. Mr. Higgins introduced her to the judge and explained that she would have to go to court again, in a month. In the meantime, he said, they had decided to send her to Midstone, where she would be under the protection of the state. He would come out to Midstone every week to see her, he said, and to give her updated reports on the progress of her case. Then he took her hand, told her not to worry and strode off down the corridor, followed by his young assistant.

Her two policemen had led her out into the street, into a cruiser, and delivered her to Midstone. She had let herself be shut into this tiny cell. She had, without a word, followed the rules of her new keepers.

The first day she was in her cell, her first afternoon at Midstone, she had had two visitors. The director of the prison had accompanied Mr. Higgins to the west wing and let him into Laura's cell, waiting outside as the lawyer conferred with his client. Although Mr. Higgins had patiently explained that Laura was at Midstone for her own protection, she had stolidly refused to answer any of his questions. Finally he had given up, called the director into the cell and asked her to speak to Laura.

The director, a matronly, brown-haired woman in her late forties, had also tried to put Laura at her ease, explaining that Laura wasn't really a prisoner and that, as soon as it was time for her trial, she would be taken back to Hartford. The director also explained that Laura had the whole west wing to herself, because it was closed off for repairs and alterations. Laura made no response and finally the director, too, had given up, and she and Mr. Higgins had left Laura alone in her cell.

That evening Laura's dinner tray was returned to the kitchen untouched.

THERE WAS A rattle of keys in the lock and the guard entered her cell to collect her lunch tray. It was the guard who had surprised her into speaking, the one who had left the cigarette Laura was enjoying as she thought about the past three weeks. Laura looked at the guard's uniform and noticed she wore a small, plastic name tag. Anna Ronstein, it said.

"Thank you for the cigarettes, Miss Ronstein," Laura said shyly.

"Call me Anna," the guard said with a smile. "Here, I brought you a pack for yourself." She set the cigarettes on the table, then turned her attention to the lunch tray. "Well, this is an improvement," she said as she saw the empty plates.

"It—it was good," the prisoner responded, smiling with the guard. For three weeks, Laura had eaten only one meal a day. Her fasting and her vow of silence had been broken, and Laura was glad of both the companionship of the guard and the pleasant feeling of a comfortably full stomach.

Anna stayed and talked to her for about an hour. As she picked up the tray and headed for the door of the cell, Laura timidly asked her if she would carry a message to the director.

"Sure thing," Anna said, knowing the director would be pleased at the change in Laura's behavior. "What do you want me to tell her?"

Laura swallowed nervously. "Ask her if . . . tell her I would like to talk to my lawyer."

Anna left the cell, humming quietly. Since Laura's arrival at Midstone the guards had been speculating about her guilt. As time had passed the question of guilt or innocence had become secondary: they realized that Laura's silence could only prejudice her chances in court. Even the best lawyer in the world could not prepare his case properly without his client's assistance.

MR. HIGGINS RESPONDED immediately to the director's call. At six o'clock that evening he was sitting in his client's cell, once again reviewing the events at Silver Farm. As he listened to Laura talk he realized that he believed totally in her innocence. No longer would he be satisfied with trying to obtain a light sentence. He made the decision to enter a plea of not guilty on his client's behalf. He would go back to his office and call the judge to tell him of the changed plea.

As he drove back to New York he thought of the

young journalist friend of Laura's, Ross Montclair. He remembered their last conversation and decided to call the journalist as soon as he'd spoken to the judge. He looked at his watch and stepped on the gas. He'd have to hurry if he wanted to catch the judge in his office—he always left his chambers promptly at eight-thirty.

He kept his eyes on the road as he fiddled with the radio, trying to find some pleasant music. As he listened to the stations his twisting fingers were locating, Mr. Higgins sighed regretfully. He knew he had set himself an almost impossible task—to convince a jury, twelve normal, everyday people, that his client was innocent. He could imagine the absurdity of his remarks: "Try to forget, ladies and gentlemen of the jury, try to forget that my client was alone at Silver Farm when this unfortunate incident occurred. Ignore the fact that she purchased the poison, and pretend no one told you she is the sole heir to an estate worth one million dollars. . . ."

Higgins snapped the radio off impatiently. *If only we had more evidence*, he thought for the hundredth time. *If only someone else had a motive.* He would call the judge anyway, he decided, and discuss the situation.

He parked his car about a block from his office and walked quickly back to the old, brownstone building. As he climbed the steps to the main door a figure separated itself from the shadows and held out an arm to bar his way. Surprised, Higgins stopped and turned to see who was there.

"Mr. Higgins," Ross Montclair's voice said from the shadows, "I have to talk to you!"

Higgins sighed. "All right, Mr. Montclair. Come along inside." As they climbed the stairs to the fourth floor Higgins told Ross about his decision to call the judge. He glanced at his watch. It was eight o'clock: he'd made good time on the highway. They walked down the hallway to his office. Higgins produced his keys and swung the door open.

As he ushered his guest in, he glanced curiously at his desk. It was covered with messages, all in the neat hand of his secretary and all saying the same thing: "Ross Montclair called; please return his call; urgent." The eleventh message had been taken at five minutes to six, and the word "urgent" was underlined four times.

Higgins turned to his guest. "Well, Ross, I take it you have something you want to talk about. What can I do for you?"

Silently, Ross handed Zizi's photographs to the lawyer. Higgins studied them for a few moments, set them on his desk and reached for the phone.

Ross paced the office while Higgins talked. Finally the lawyer hung up and turned to his guest.

"It's all set, Mr. Montclair. The judge will see us tomorrow morning at eight. I'll hold onto these photographs for you—they'll be kept in my safe for the night. We've got a lot of work to do—the trial date is only a week away, and it's too late for a postponement. We'll just have to hope that the judge will agree to a little informal confrontation after he sees these photos."

Ross looked at the lawyer, a smile beginning to ease the deeply etched lines of strain on his face. "You mean you think we have a chance?"

The lawyer put his hand on Ross's shoulder. "Mr. Montclair, I am not a gambling man by nature. But I'll bet you a trip for two to Paris that this case will never go to court." He opened a drawer of his desk, took out a pipe, filled it with tobacco and carefully lighted it.

"Meet me here tomorrow morning at half-past seven, all right?"

Ross nodded. "And, Mr. Higgins—"

"Not now, Ross. If you'll excuse me, I have a lot of work to do between now and tomorrow morning."

Grinning happily, Ross left the lawyer's office and walked the eighteen blocks to his hotel.

Chapter 15

Four days later Ross accompanied the lawyer to the judge's chambers for the second time. A lot had happened in those four days. Ross had been working around the clock, and so had Higgins and his assistant. Their work had been worth it: as Ross walked into the judge's large, comfortable office, he was imagining how Laura would react when she was given her freedom.

The judge's room seemed to be full of people. The clerk was running back and forth, fetching coffee and chairs for the guests. There were actually four rooms in the chambers: this large one, a private office, a reception room and another small room with no windows. Ross knew that the judge had planned this "informal confrontation" carefully, and that Zizi of the magic fingers was in one of the rooms, with an interpreter. He also knew Phyllis Baker was being kept somewhere, and several other people from Silver Farm would be present.

As Ross took a seat Judge Roberts entered the room, a large, yellow file in his right hand. He sat behind his desk, motioned to the clerk and asked him to place two comfortable armchairs in front of the desk. The clerk obeyed, then went to fetch the first "witness." He reappeared a moment later and announced, "Mr. Robert Collins."

The judge asked Robert Collins to take a seat. "I'm sorry to have bothered you, Mr. Collins. You'd planned to leave, hadn't you?"

Collins glanced curiously around the room, then sat in an armchair. He crossed his long legs. "That's right. This is all a bit inconvenient—I've got a plane to catch." He glanced at his watch in its heavy gold case. "I don't have long to spend here."

"We'll expedite this as quickly as possible," the judge promised. "You planned on leaving the country?"

"I've got business in Europe . . . a travel agency. Oh, well! If I'm late, my assistant will replace me."

Collins's voice was clear and nonchalant, and he seemed to be relaxed. Ross noticed that he was careful to look the judge in the eye as often as possible.

Collins pulled out a package of cigarettes. "Do you smoke, Your Honor?"

"No, thanks."

"Do you mind if I do? It's a bad habit, I know, but I can't seem to shake it."

Judge Roberts nodded and placed an ashtray in front of his guest.

As Collins lighted his cigarette, the judge buried his nose in his papers. His gray hair and peaceful face were misleading. Although he seemed to be a dreamy man, a cluster of sharp wrinkles around his eyes told of his piercing intelligence.

Without looking up at Robert Collins, he flipped

through the yellow file folder. Collins shifted his weight in the chair. The prolonged silence was beginning, it seemed, to make him nervous.

Finally he could stand the silence no longer, and he asked, "Are you finally convinced that that woman, who took advantage of my brother, is really guilty?"

"My investigation is not quite over yet."

"But I thought . . . all the newspapers announced this morning the trial was about to begin."

"It will begin soon," the judge said without looking up.

"Your Honor, my brother's death must be avenged. I won't rest until his murderer is brought to justice!"

"Mr. Collins, the courts will see to it. You can trust them."

"But we're dealing with a maniac! A woman who would poison a man with weed killer has to be crazy! And she seems to think she can get away with anything!"

"Do you know her?" the judge asked.

"Me? No, of course not. I've just been reading what the papers are saying. They seem to agree with me—and I don't blame them."

"Relax, Mr. Collins," Judge Roberts said soothingly. "I can understand your brother's death was a shock, and that you feel bitter toward the accused. But try to keep calm. Justice will triumph."

"I hope so," Collins muttered, a little chastened.

The judge put his elbows on his desk and leaned toward Collins. "In your statement, you said you hadn't spoken to your brother in a good number of years."

"I left home twelve years ago and I haven't seen him

since then—except on TV or in the magazines. My brother was a somebody, a star all over the world."

The judge raised his hand to silence Robert's belated elegy. "I know, I know, Mr. Collins. And did you know anyone who worked for him?"

"How could I? I was thousands of miles away." He stubbed out his cigarette—a little too violently, Ross thought excitedly.

"Harriet Alvin, the cook, for example?"

"No."

The judge pushed down an intercom button on his desk and spoke quietly into the speaker. "Send in the second witness. I've almost finished with Mr. Collins."

Judge Roberts continued to browse through the papers in his file, but Collins was intrigued. He turned around as the door swung open. Phyllis Baker halted on the threshold as her eyes met his. In the silence that followed, a current seemed to pass between them suddenly. Then the tension eased as Collins stood up.

"Hello, miss," he said in a neutral voice.

She nodded in his direction, then looked at the judge.

"Hello, Miss Baker. Please be seated." He indicated the other armchair. "You can sit down now, too, Mr. Collins," the judge suggested dryly.

Collins did as he was told. He stared into space, seemingly unaware of the woman who was sitting next to him. She was dressed in a simply tailored gray suit with a plain, white blouse. She looked the picture of innocence and reserve, with her hair pulled back severely from her scrubbed, open face.

"Miss Baker, do you know Mr. Robert Collins?" the judge asked.

Miss Baker shook her head without bothering to glance at the man beside her. He, however, was more loquacious.

"I must say, this is a privilege. I've heard a lot about you, Miss Baker, since the beginning of the case. And if I might, I'd like to thank you for the devotion you showed for my poor brother."

Miss Baker smiled weakly. "It was an honor to work for him. I was very hurt by what happened."

"His murderer will have her due!"

"That's exactly what I was coming to," the judge cut in. "I asked you both to come here to compare your statements. They seem to cover all the angles. You, Mr. Collins, are asking for civil damages—that is, your brother's estate. You, Miss Baker, are accusing the widow of having tried to hide a murder behind a suicide. Is that correct?"

"That's what my statement suggests," Phyllis Baker said dryly.

"I don't want a suggestion, Miss Baker, I want a yes or no answer. Are you, or are you not, accusing the widow of trying to mask a murder?"

"Yes, sir, I am," Phyllis Baker answered, her face going suddenly pale.

"Mr. Collins?"

"Correct, Your Honor."

The judge leaned over and spoke into the intercom once more. "Please send in the next witness."

Neither Phyllis Baker nor Robert Collins showed any emotion when the door opened. Neither of them even glanced at the door. Phyllis Baker looked at the floor; Robert Collins was gazing idly out the window.

"Come in, Zizi. Don't be shy," the judge said kindly.

"I'd like to introduce two witnesses for the prosecution: Robert Collins and Phyllis Baker."

Zizi took a few tentative steps into the judge's chambers, followed by a birdlike woman with a stenographer's pad.

"I asked a translator to help us out," the judge explained to the people in the room. "Zizi is French, and she doesn't speak a work of English. Miss Jones here will translate everything for you as we talk."

"I know this man!" Zizi burst out suddenly. Then she turned to the translator and said excitedly, "Don't bother translating. He speaks French."

"I do as well," the judge said to Zizi in French. Then he explained to her that Miss Jones would translate anyway, so that everyone would understand. Unnerved by all the people in the room, Zizi bit her lip. "Please continue, miss," Judge Roberts said coaxingly. "You were saying you were acquainted with this man?"

Twisting her fingers nervously, Zizi turned once again to Robert Collins. "It was back in France, on the train to the Riviera, a few months ago. You're the man who wanted to meet Delia Marston!"

A look of surprise replaced Collins's blank stare. "I don't know what you're talking about," he said haughtily.

Scenting a battle, Zizi became more assured. "How could you have forgotten our encounter? You were the guy who was absolutely sure Miss Dolan was some film star. You were so persistent I finally told you exactly who Laura—I mean, Miss Dolan—really was. I even told you she was a designer at Leonardo's. Now do you remember?"

Robert Collins drew himself up in the armchair. "I'm

afraid you're mistaken, Miss . . . uh, Zizi. Perhaps I remind you of someone you once met, and you noticed a resemblance—"

"You're the one who takes advantage of resemblances," Zizi broke in excitedly. "That's *your* trick, not mine. That's how you managed to learn so much about Laura—"

"What's this woman talking about?" Collins interrupted angrily, looking at the judge. "Your Honor, I don't have any time to waste. Please take down my formal statement. This Zizi woman is making a serious mistake. She thinks I'm someone else. I swear I've never met her in my life."

"Just as you swear you've never met Miss Baker?" the judge asked, raising an eyebrow.

Before Collins had a chance to ask the judge what he meant, Zizi pointed a finger at Phyllis Baker. "Just a minute!" Zizi said, staring excitedly at the nurse. "This is the lady, judge! This lady was with Mr. Collins when I took the picture. I didn't recognize her at first because I've never seen her dressed like this. But I'm sure this is the same woman!"

"Have you lost your mind?" Phyllis Baker's voice was cold and angry. "I wasn't on any train to Nice."

"No, you weren't on the train. But you *were* in Nice, hanging onto this man's arm. I recognize you now—even though you did look a lot happier back then than you do today."

"How dare you—"

"Your Honor, I demand you put a stop to these incoherent ramblings," Robert Collins stormed. "Otherwise I'll—I'll charge her with slander."

"Slander? Why would you do that?" The judge

laughed quietly. "Is there anything slanderous about accusing someone of being seen with a pretty woman?"

"I won't have anyone calling me a liar," Collins sputtered.

"Be patient. Let's try to get to the bottom of this, shall we? Now, Zizi, when did all this running around on trains take place?"

"It was Laura's birthday, sir—Your Honor, I mean."

Judge Roberts smiled. "Right. Zizi . . . when is Laura's birthday, by the way?"

Ross grinned as Zizi blushed. "April third, sir—I mean, Your Honor," the Parisian answered.

"And you and Mrs. Collins—Miss Dolan—went to Nice, and you, uh, encountered Mr. Collins there?"

"Yes, Your Honor."

"That's not true!" Robert Collins shouted, rising from his chair.

"Sit down, Mr. Collins!" the judge snapped. "Are you claiming that Zizi is lying?"

"She's mistaken." Phyllis answered the judge's question in a nervous voice, then qualified her answer. "At least, the parts about me are a mistake."

"And she's lying about me, too," Collins said, trying to keep his voice calm.

The judge gave him a disapproving look. "Do you deny you were with Phyllis Baker in Nice last April?'

"Yes! How many times do I have to—"

"Mr. Collins, would you kindly keep your temper," the judge said severely. "Don't forget where you are. There are certain excesses I won't tolerate."

"Yes, Your Honor. I'm sorry. But this—this preposterous story upsets me."

"Unfortunately for you," the judge retorted, "this story, as you call it, is based on solid evidence."

"Evidence?" Collins repeated dumbly. "What kind of evidence? How could anyone prove I was on a train, anyway?"

The judge waited until Collins became less agitated. Then he reached under the pile of papers on his desk and removed the yellow file. He carefully extracted an enlargement of Zizi's snapshot, and held it so the two witnesses for the prosecution could see it clearly.

"Do you recognize yourselves?" the judge asked gently.

The silence was incriminating. Phyllis Baker seemed to realize it, and said, in a tiny voice, "That doesn't prove we were in Nice that day. That picture could have been taken anywhere."

Judge Roberts looked at her sharply. "Are you admitting you knew Mr. Collins at the time?" the judge asked her quietly. "You've denied it repeatedly—under oath, I might add. Why is that?"

Phyllis Baker didn't answer. Her reserve crumbled, and she hid her face in her hands and sobbed.

Robert Collins tried valiantly to reassert his crumbling defenses. "Your Honor, please. Don't we have the right to a private life? Our relationship doesn't concern anyone."

"That's where you're wrong, Mr. Collins—your relationship concerns all of us. You lied to the court, to the district attorney and to me—and because of your lies, an innocent woman has been hurt." The judge pressed a button on his desk, then continued. "Laura Collins was set up—she's nothing but a convenient scapegoat for your selfish, warped schemes. If she were convicted of murder, her late husband's fortune would go to his next of kin—you, Mr. Collins. It was a clever plan and you almost pulled it off. But your 'perfect crime' had one small flaw. . . ."

Robert Collins's self-assurance disappeared as the door to the judge's office opened once more. He looked up and froze. Four uniformed policemen stood in the doorway.

Chapter 16

Phyllis Baker was not the strong-willed, detached professional she had appeared to be. Two hours after her confrontation with Judge Roberts she made a full, and very emotional, confession.

Robert Collins was less cooperative, and maintained a disdainful silence for three days. But during those three days the police were busy checking on Phyllis Baker's story. By the time Robert Collins confessed, the detectives had all the evidence they needed to convict him. The details Phyllis Baker had given them set them on Collins's trail. Little by little, a sinister portrait began to emerge, and this information shed light on the death of Sidney Collins.

From the day of his birth, Robert Collins had brought misery to his family. His mother had died on the delivery table, moments before Robert's birth. James, his father, had mourned his birth. Robert had found no favor in their hearts and, in retaliation, his own heart had hardened.

The Collins family lived in barely suppressed discord for sixteen years. Sidney, then just coming of age, was enrolled in the Conservatory; Robert was a rebellious high-school student. His pranks grew increasingly vengeful and frequent. After one particularly heinous incident, which nearly turned to tragedy, James exiled his younger son from the family home, disowned him and thereafter denied his existence.

Those who met the young drifter saw the scion of a wealthy family, a golden boy, a charmer. He was good-looking, silver-tongued, urbane. But his charm and good looks cloaked a soul totally devoid of scruples. The heartlessness that had been his birthright was coming to maturity.

The young outcast began drifting, living from hand to mouth. He used his charm and lordly manner to stay alive, easily convincing his gullible victims to support impossible schemes, all involving large sums of money. Until he was sixteen, Robert had existed only for the day of James's death, the day the Collins will was read. Now the estate, in its entirety, would go to Sidney. For several years Robert wandered the world, scheming to be reinstated in his father's good graces. James refused a reconciliation. He died when his younger son was twenty-two, and Sidney was sole heir.

Robert's lifelong grudge against his more fortunate brother deepened. But his devious mind followed what was, for it, a logical path. Robert approached his older brother, attempting to ingratiate himself once again into the family. Sidney had mourned his mother's death and had, like James, held Robert responsible for her loss. He knew his brother's destructive nature. He knew Robert had not grieved when James died. Sidney refused to meet with Robert, and from that moment on denied his younger brother's existence.

But Robert refused to give up. Several years later his older brother married. Robert viewed Patricia as a second chance. She accepted him, let herself be persuaded by him and lent him money. And she talked to him kindly, trying desperately to reform the young man. Robert saw his opportunity and tried to lead her into a sordid affair. Unable to cope, Patricia confessed her problem to Sidney. The family connection was severed immediately—and forever.

For eight years Robert stayed away from his brother. But he had not forgotten, and in his mind he was planning his revenge. He traveled all over the world, never staying long in any one place, never becoming emotionally involved with anyone. He was waiting for the right moment, the moment of retaliation. The thought of the Collins family money was like an eternal beacon, motivating his every move. He had been scorned, degraded by his brother. His life had been a futile wasteland of unfulfilled dreams. He lived only for that one moment, when the fortune his brother disdained would be his. Knowing the odds, Robert patiently waited.

The moment came. Sidney had a car accident. His wife was killed; his life hung by a thread. To Robert, it appeared as though, at long last, his patience had paid off. He would cash in. He was his brother's sole heir. His windfall would be twice as sweet: his father's estate would fall into his hands—and so would Sidney's. The irony pleased him.

In a few days, or weeks perhaps, Sidney would die. And Robert would be rich. All he had to do was wait.

But Robert couldn't wait. Thirty-seven years of frustrated dreams had taught him his lesson: Lady Luck needed a gentle nudge, sometimes, or her favors would land in someone else's lap. Robert needed someone to give that nudge, a partner. And he knew exactly whom he wanted.

Her name was Phyllis Baker. She was a registered nurse, and almost forty when they had met. Robert had been hurt, and was taken, unconscious, to a hospital in Milwaukee. When he came to she was at his side. Robert had begun talking to her, telling her his version of his life story. The nurse, who led a painfully normal life, had fallen desperately in love with her cosmopolitan patient. She told him everything—how she'd managed to save enough money, by living frugally, to maybe someday sail around the world. How she feared life had passed her by. And how frightened she was of her loneliness. Cynically, Robert had promised to save her from herself. Then he had disappeared.

When he called on her for help, she responded immediately. To her co-workers and acquaintances she was a quiet, repressed, self-contained woman. Yet there was another Phyllis Baker, a woman who lost total control of her will when Robert Collins spoke. He elaborated on the stories he had told her in the hospital, and invented a scenario that showed him in the best possible light. He convinced her that he had been the victim of a family injustice, then he sent her to his brother's bedside.

Sidney was in a hospital in Switzerland. Phyllis had no trouble following Robert's orders: to be hired as Sidney's personal nurse. She had a briefcase full of qualifications and recommendations, and no one ever questioned her claim that she had been sent by several of the patient's American friends. She was confident in her ability to please Robert. All he wanted was information. She need do no wrong, she need break no sacred trust or ethical code. She was innocent—and unaware of the power Robert had over her.

For the next few weeks Sidney existed in that no-man's-land between life and death. The doctors offered little hope for his survival. Each afternoon, like a trained spy, Phyllis sent a detailed report of her patient's progress to her accomplice.

Then, suddenly, Sidney came out of his coma. He responded well to all the tests the medical men subjected him to; there was even talk of a complete recovery. The doctors were hopeful, and the music world was jubilant. But two people were shattered by Sidney's progress: Phyllis Baker and Robert Collins.

After lengthy consultations, the doctors agreed that Sidney was stable enough to journey to a rest home in the hills north of Nice. The gentle climate would favor his recovery, they decided, and the countryside would be good for his depression. It was normal for him to be depressed: he had lost his wife, he had almost died. But now he must begin to live again.

Phyllis Baker, faithful nurse and companion, accompanied the musician to his new home. Discreet, self-effacing, efficient, she had quickly become indispensable. She was gaining his trust, becoming an accepted—and necessary—part of his life. Robert was beginning to relax, and even spoke vaguely of marriage. Phyllis lived in hope.

As the days went by the musician's body began to gain strength, but his mind seemed to slip deeper into depression. He refused to believe in his own recovery, and as his thoughts grew more morbid, he began to wish for his death. Then, suddenly, he summoned his lawyer. Together they rewrote his will. The dying man began to make plans to leave his entire estate to a retirement home for elderly musicians. Then he decided to return to his home in Connecticut.

For Robert, the new will was the final injustice. He had been done out of what he thought of as his rightful inheritance once—he would not let it happen again. But how could he prevent it? At a loss for ideas, he called Phyllis and set up a rendezvous with her. He would take the train to Nice, and she would meet him there.

As Robert walked along the platform in the Paris station, hurrying to catch his train, he came face to face with Laura Dolan. Her appearance was such a shock that, after a few steps, he stopped dead in his tracks and stared. She looked so much like Sidney's late wife. . . . And in his scheming mind, a plan began to take shape. The idea would take time to ripen, and many details would have to be worked out, but it just might work. . . .

As the train headed south, Robert thought feverishly, trying to work out a strategy. Thanks to the scatter-brained, unsuspecting Zizi, he had managed to learn Laura's name, and where she worked. For a man who had lived by his wits all his life, setting a trap for Miss Laura Dolan was easy. It required only a little time and some kind of bait, something so farfetched that no one could doubt its reality or resist its allure.

Robert began to work out the details of his plan. Laura would, unknowingly, play the starring role. If he could bring Laura and Sidney together . . . . Once Sidney saw Laura, he would be unable to deny—or resist—her resemblance to his wife. Then Robert could let nature take her course. But nothing could begin until

Sidney and Laura were brought together. He had to lure Laura to Silver Farm. Then, with a little help from Phyllis, Robert could easily do what was needed.

He met Phyllis in Nice. When he told her of his plan, she was shocked. "No," she protested. "It's crazy, it's wrong and I won't have any part of it."

But her arguments were soon silenced. She was no match for the irrepressible Robert. He repeated all the arguments he had used to convince Phyllis to travel to Switzerland. He claimed the inheritance was his, and he painted a picture of a cruel and scheming family, trying to deprive him of what was his by right. And his brother was dying anyway. Life had lost all joy for him. Robert's plan would only hasten the inevitable. Still Phyllis protested.

Then Robert played his trump card. "It's the only way we can be together," he told Phyllis. "It's him or me. If you don't help, I'll have nothing . . . and I'll vanish." Phyllis knew he meant it. She agreed to help him with his plan.

The two schemers strolled through the sunshine in Nice, working out the details of the trap. Then Phyllis returned to her patient, and Robert got to work. There were a lot of people who owed him favors, and he had no trouble finding a "friend" to play the part of Hermes Azopardi. A fake contract was drawn up and the gullible Leonardo fell for it—and so did Laura. Lady Luck blessed Robert's endeavors, and Laura was anxious to swallow the bait with which he set his trap. She was ready to move, and no date was too soon. Robert arranged for her to sail on the S. S. *La Reine* with his brother.

Everything had been arranged down to the smallest

detail: the ticket, the table in the dining room, the deck chair. The trickiest bit was accomplished, and Robert began to relax. Phyllis would see to the rest.

"So you see," said Inspector Finch, gazing into his glass of brandy, "Miss Baker's trump card was the alibi she set up for herself."

The room was silent except for the scratching of pens and the hum of tape recorders. Finch had agreed to give a special interview to a group of French journalists. Ross had set the interview up, and he relaxed in a comfortable armchair, sipping at some of the inspector's fine brandy.

"She wasn't even in the house when Sidney Collins died. Everything pointed to Miss Dolan. In a way, Sidney did commit suicide—he picked up the poisoned glass and drank from it."

Finch gazed again at his brandy. Apparently deciding it was safe, he took a swallow.

"Collins had a glass of water before going to bed—it was one of his habits. A pitcherful was sitting on his night table, and all Miss Baker had to do was stir the poison into it. His wife gave him a glass of water with his medication . . . he took the pill, swallowed the water and had another glass a short time later. His death was quick . . . and probably painless.

"The next morning Phyllis Baker, with the housekeeper and the chauffeur as witnesses, 'discovered' what had happened. She immediately did two things. She left a bottle of sleeping pills on the rug near Collins's hand. Her idea was to implicate Mrs. Collins by making us think the wife had faked his suicide. The nurse depended on the fact that the autopsy would show he hadn't died of an overdose of sleeping pills, but of a massive amount of weed killer. The new evidence would lead us straight to Miss Dolan. Of course, she made sure an autopsy would be performed by suggesting, right from the start, that something was odd.

"The second thing she did was to clean out the pitcher and the glass. The housekeeper was a young girl, inexperienced. She was shocked—so Phyllis could act freely. Almost an hour went by before the doctor arrived. She figured she'd covered all the angles."

"But that still leaves some uncertainty," one of the journalists objected. "Mrs. Collins could have come back to her husband's room, discovered his body and alerted the doctor before Phyllis had the chance to clean up the room"

Finch shrugged his shoulders. "That's the calculated risk all criminals have to face . . . the unexpected. But Collins and Baker decided to risk it—and they damn near got away with it.

"The only thing they couldn't take into consideration was a fluke—a fluke that had occurred months before, when a sightseeing Parisian pointed her camera lens at a happy couple leaving a jewelry shop. No one thought twice about that picture at the time, but it saved Laura Collins from a life in prison."

Chapter 17

The abrupt knock on the door made Roger Parent drop his pencil and look up. "Ross! Where have you been keeping yourself? Come in."

Ross sat in the leather armchair by the window and gazed out onto the street below. He dug a cigarette out of his pocket and absently searched his pockets for matches. After a moment he gave up, and accepted his friend's lighter.

"Bourbon? Scotch?" Roger offered.

"No, thanks, I've just got a minute."

"Your last day in town?"

"That's right. I'm taking the plane tonight."

Roger looked surprised. "Tonight! Why are you in such a hurry? This is a beautiful city—you should stay for a while, take a vacation."

"Roger, I haven't touched a typewriter in three weeks. The boss gave me the time off because of my scoop about . . . about Laura, but I can't stretch that out forever. And to tell you the truth, I miss the grind."

"How's Laura?" Roger asked quietly.

Taking a puff of his cigarette, Ross answered coolly,

"Not bad. She spent some time with some people in New Jersey and she seems to be feeling better. Her friend Zizi—what a woman she is! Anyway, she managed to talk Leonardo into giving her some extra vacation time to help Laura get back on her feet again. Now Laura's better than ever. She's set up shop at the Waldorf Astoria and her phone hasn't stopped ringing. She's a celebrity and she can't get a moment's peace with all the people knocking at her door."

"Well, that's quite a change from her last residence," Roger said sardonically. "Poor Laura! But she does deserve a break after that ordeal."

"Poor? The heiress to the Collins fortune? That's not exactly the word I'd use."

"Did she go back to Silver Farm?"

"No. She says it brings back too many bad memories. She's thinking of selling the house."

Both men smoked in silence for a minute. Then, carefully, Roger asked, "Are you leaving for good?"

"Yes. What would I do here? New York's fine for you—you've got the illustrious title of official foreign correspondant."

"Oh, it's not all glory, believe me." Roger tried halfheartedly to defend himself.

"In any case, I was glad you were here. You helped us out a lot and I'm grateful to you."

"Oh, it's nothing," Roger said with a wave of his hand. Expressions of emotion made him feel ill at ease. He changed the subject. "What about Laura? Is she going back to Paris, too?"

"Laura's too busy being a millionaire heiress. From what I hear, it's a full-time occupation." There was more than a touch of bitterness in the journalist's voice.

Roger cleared his throat nervously. "It's funny, you know."

"What's funny?"

"The way this story finally ended."

"You mean Laura's story? I think it has a great ending. It's the triumph of good over evil—the perfect moral tale. The guilty ones are punished, the victim gets her revenge. And she also gets a fabulous sum of money to console her for her suffering. She can finally take her place in the ranks of the earth's inheritors, who do exactly what they want to, always. Isn't that the proper ending to any romantic story?"

"I thought you loved Laura," Roger said, trying to temper Ross's irony.

Ross stared out at the sidewalks of New York, watching the traffic. "Of course I loved her," he said in a distant voice. "I even thought she loved me enough to spend the rest of her life with me. Well, that was an illusion, the dream of a boy who never grew up!"

"You're too hard on yourself, Ross. Why not go ahead with your plans?"

Ross smiled wryly. "Sure, Roger, it would be easy. Can you imagine me marrying the heir to a million bucks?"

"Ross, will you kindly stop talking about money for a minute? Think about Laura. I've seen you two together, and it looked like it was working."

"Are you nuts? You know it's impossible!" Ross shot back. "Laura is Mrs. Collins now, Roger—the fabulously rich heiress and the star of the scandal that shook the nation. Every door is open to her. She'll marry an Onassis or a Rockefeller—"

"Or an Italian duke, a Spanish count or a German

prince. But what if she'd rather have a reporter from a French television station?"

"How could I agree to that? Face it, Roger, I could never be the kind of man who lives off his wife. Every time I gave her a present, I would know she could get the same thing—only ten times better than what I could afford. I want to work together with her, even if it means hard times. I want to make a future with her, really make it, the two of us working together. All of that's impossible with the widow of Sidney Collins. I'd be marrying a million dollars—not a wife. Can't you see that?"

Roger didn't answer. He put out his cigarette and asked gently, "And what does Laura think about all this?"

"Laura?" Ross shrugged his shoulders. "She's taken to her identity like a fish to water. It fits her like a glove. She gives interviews, poses for pictures, calls in bankers and lawyers. You'd think she'd been doing it all her life." He lighted another cigarette.

"Did it ever occur to you, Ross, that maybe that's not Laura's fault? All those people, and the bankers and lawyers, they haven't got your scruples. *They* call *her*—because she's got money. She can't help it if they're getting down on their knees to her. What do you expect her to do?"

Ross was unimpressed by Roger's reasoning. "Well, as far as I can see, she hasn't said no to any of them yet. She loves it! Yesterday I couldn't even get in to see her because some banker was there, offering her some kind of deal. It didn't take her long to learn how to be rich and famous! I'm afraid Laura and I aren't on the same wavelength anymore."

"Does she know you're going back to France?" Roger asked.

"Of course she knows." Ross glanced at his watch. "I'm going to see her now—to tell her goodbye."

Roger stood up. "Can I drop you off at her hotel?" he asked.

Ross nervously stubbed out his cigarette. "Sure," he answered. "You can even wait for me. I don't expect to be there for more than five minutes. When you don't have money, your interviews with Laura are short and painless."

"Have you read tonight's papers?" Roger asked as they walked down the stairs to his car.

"I haven't had time," Ross answered abruptly. He got into the car and slammed the door.

As they pulled up at Laura's hotel a few moments later, Roger asked, "I'll wait for you in the bar, okay?"

"All right," Ross agreed, and headed for the door.

AT THE WALDORF Astoria Hotel, Mrs. Laura Collins was considered a VIP. She was showered with every attention the grand old establishment could provide. When Ross presented himself at the desk and informed the clerk that he had an appointment with Laura, he was greeted with much bowing and scraping. The clerk telephoned upstairs and informed Ross that he was, indeed, expected. Ross entered the elevator.

During the short ride to her floor, he told himself to be detached. But once he reached her door, he halted, his courage deserting him. Finally he brought himself to knock on her door.

That clear voice, as familiar as his own, responded immediately to his knock.

"I knew you'd come," Laura said, smiling with pleasure as she opened the door. "But you're a little late, Ross—I was beginning to worry."

She was wearing a plain black suit, elegantly cut but stylish in its simplicity. She bent over and snapped a suitcase shut.

"Are you leaving?" he asked. He glanced around the room. It looked like a cyclone had passed through it.

"Yes. I've had enough of New York."

"Really? Blasé already?"

"Not blasé—fed up with all these people."

"And what's going to happen to all your journalist and photographer friends?" he teased bitterly. "And the bankers and lawyers and . . . ."

"They're the least of my worries. They'll just have to find someone else to prey on, I guess."

She took a deep breath and sat on her last suitcase, fighting to get it shut. Then she turned to Ross and gave him a cheerful look. This Laura was a far cry from the wan, desperate girl he had found locked in a prison cell. Her cheeks had filled out and her eyes sparkled. She looked like the same girl he'd loved in Paris, before this whole mad adventure began. But she wasn't the same. A million dollars separated him from her now—she was a stranger to him.

"Would it be indiscreet to ask you where you're go-ing? Rome? California? Or maybe Jamaica?"

Laura laughed. "It sounds like you've taken a job with a travel agency. I'm not going to any of those places. I'm going back."

"Back? Back where?"

"Home, stupid, France. Remember? I live in Paris."

"Paris?" Ross repeated, his mouth suddenly dry.

"You heard me. What's so unusual about that? Can't I go home?"

"Sure, you can go home. You can go anywhere you

want, Israel, India . . . you can go around the world if you feel like it."

She shook her head. "It might be nice—if that's what I wanted. But I want to go home, and Paris is good enough for me."

Ross stood in the middle of the impersonal hotel room, staring at the woman he had loved. He opened his mouth several times, but finally shut it in frustration.

"I get the feeling my plans don't please you, darling Ross."

"I'm not your darling Ross!" he snapped, taking a step back from her "I wish you wouldn't call me that."

"But I've always called you that. You were my darling Ross when I was eight, and fourteen and sixteen and eighteen—"

"Well, you're not fourteen and sixteen and eighteen anymore—and I'm not your darling Ross. We're too big for that—I mean, we're adults."

Ignoring his reply, Laura came closer, inexorably closer. Ross tried to step back, but he had no room. His back was to the wall.

"Kiss me, Ross."

"No!"

"You don't want to kiss me?"

"No, I *won't* kiss you."

"But you still love me?"

"Yes, damn you, I still love you."

"And you want to marry me?"

"No!"

"Why not?"

"Because you've got too much money!"

"Well, I've—"

"And I don't have any. I'm like everybody else—I have to work to earn a living."

"Me, too, of course."

He stared at her incredulously. "Come on, Laura, stop playing humble. You're a solid-gold security now. If you want husbands you can get them by the shovelful."

Laura returned his stare. "Come on, Ross, enough's enough. Do you want to talk seriously for once?"

She walked up to him and took his hand. "Don't get mad, Ross. It won't solve anything. You came in here angry, ready to fight, and look what happened. This is silly—two adults, as you so bravely called us, quarreling over our wedding day."

"Forget it, Laura. We can't get married now."

"Why not? Are you afraid I won't be able to find a job? Do you think I'll be a drag on the family finances?"

He gave her a withering look. "You know, Laura, your jokes are getting kind of tasteless these days."

"Thanks a lot, darling Ross. I suppose you'd blame it on the company I keep." She paused, considering. "Why can't we pick up where we left off? Is there another woman?"

"Don't be stupid."

She gave him a sly look. "What about Sonia?"

"Sonia never counted and you know it. She was only a friend, just a—"

"An interlude?" Laura suggested.

"Whatever. There was never really anyone but you," he added grudgingly.

"So?"

"So I won't marry the widow of Sidney Collins!"

"You're not being reasonable, Ross. I've already told

you, more than once. I was never Sidney's wife, and you know what I mean. So what's the problem?"

"All that damned money he left you!" Ross stormed. "I won't touch it. I live off what I earn, not what someone else leaves behind."

"But won't you let me help you?"

"Never!"

"You never said that before. We both agreed I'd work. You said we'd live like every other young couple, sharing everything: our dreams, our hopes, our ambitions and our finances."

He stared at her furiously. "Don't turn the knife in the wound. Sure, that's what I was counting on back when you had your hair down to your waist and wore a pair of mended jeans."

"They weren't mended. They were just a little worn around the edges."

"I don't care what shape they were in. Now everything's over."

"But why, Ross? Why is everything over? Because I've just made a fantastic deal? Does that have to wreck everything?"

"Of course not, stupid! You're pretending you don't understand anything."

"What is there to understand? Yesterday I signed a contract with that businessman who came to see me while you were waiting outside. You didn't even stay to say goodbye!"

"Your business dealings don't interest me."

She struck his shoulders with her little fists. "Would you listen to me for once, Ross Montclair? Just shut up and listen!"

Ross stared at her in amazement. "You haven't left your temper anywhere, that's for sure."

Laura smiled and calmed down. "Listen, Ross, I'm going to manage a clothing designer's studio. That guy who came to see me is an American, and he wants to start a chain of clothing stores in France. I mean a really big chain—and he asked me to organize the whole line. He likes my designs and he trusts me. Well, doesn't it sound like the right job for me? Or do you think I'm totally useless?"

"You mean . . . you mean you'd go back to working, just like before, even with all your money?"

"What money? What are you talking about?"

"Your inheritance!"

"Money, money, money—that's all you can think about. You have a one-track mind!"

"Don't you agree it's an absorbing subject?"

"Where have you been all day? You're supposed to be a reporter and you don't even read the papers. Here, take a look at this, you stubborn idiot!"

Laura picked up six newspapers and flung them angrily at Ross. He caught one on the fly and straightened out the front page. The headline jumped out at him:

WIDOW REFUSES MILLIONS

Ross read the first paragraph in disbelief.

The widow of Sidney Collins refuses to claim her inheritance. Obeying the wish of her late husband, she has signed the entire sum over to the Home for Retired Musicians.

Ross read the lines over and over again. He stood, staring stupidly at the article, until he heard Laura giggle. Finally he dropped the paper and looked up at her.

"You did that?"

She gave him a tentative smile. "Surprised?"

"No, not really. That kind of crazy thing is just like you."

"Crazy? Ross Montclair, if I were you, I'd be careful who I called crazy!"

She started to laugh, then her face grew serious. "I couldn't explain this to anyone else, Ross, but . . . that money doesn't belong to me. It's not mine to keep. It's tainted with the blood of an innocent man. I wouldn't have kept it for anything in the world. Do you understand?"

"Yes, darling, I do."

Ross reached out and took her hand. He closed his eyes and thought of home. The banks of the Seine in autumn, the sunlight reflected in the river, the leaves floating in the pools of the fountains. He kissed her hair, her cheeks, her eyelids. Quietly, gently, Ross held Laura in his arms. She was still his Laura, impulsive, impetuous . . . his.

MYSTIQUE BOOKS

Experience the warmth of love... and the threat of danger!

MYSTIQUE BOOKS are a breathless blend of romance and suspense, passion and mystery. Let them take you on journeys to exotic lands—the sunny Caribbean, the enchantment of Paris, the sinister streets of Istanbul.

MYSTIQUE BOOKS

An unforgettable reading experience.
Now... many previously published titles are once again available.
Choose from this great selection!

Don't miss any of these thrilling novels of love and adventure!

Choose from this list of exciting
MYSTIQUE BOOKS